PINS AND NEEDLES

War Angels MC

Table of Contents

Prologue
Needles
Kabul - 6 Years Ago

"How long have you been here Corporal?" The Major asked me as we stood on the edges of the base just outside of Kabul and watched the wind brush over the sand.

"Going on six months sir," I answered, clasping my hands behind my back.

"You were downtown yesterday after that suicide bomb went off?"

"Yes sir," I really didn't want to think about it. I was there helping with clean up, I thought I had heard the voice of a child from under some rubble so I started digging through, moving the chunks of cement. I finally found an arm of a little girl.

I checked for a pulse and I swear there was one there, it was weak but I felt it. I moved some more rubble and thought I had dug down enough that I could pull her out but when I tugged gently on the arm it came away not attached to the body.

"We're supposed to be here training the Afghan's, not cleaning up dead kids." The Major said angrily but there was a quiver in his voice that I hadn't heard before.

"Sir?" I said turning to look at him.

"I can't do it anymore . . ." If I had been faster, or smarter or I don't know what, but if I had been that I would have seen it coming. When I walked up to the Major I had seen his hand resting on his hand gun holstered but not secured at his thigh. I had sensed his movement but was too caught up in my own head.

Thankfully, or not I was quite a bit taller than the Major, so when he put that gun to his head and pulled the trigger I was hit in the face with brain matter and blood splatter, and instead of that bullet going into my head it creased across my collar bones, leaving a deep furrow but not killing me.

Over the next couple of years I would thank God for that, and then I would curse Him. I would also thank God for the next fix of heroin and curse Him, His mother and His grandmother when I was detoxing and going through withdrawal.

I was a fucked up individual after those two days in Kabul, I would leave the armed forces and find myself on the streets of Vancouver within a month of getting home. Now I thank God for Lo and the War Angels MC.

CHAPTER 1

Needles – Present Day

"Please Mr. Winters," I heard the voice begging Lo for something, but didn't expect what I saw when I walked into his office. "My brother is only eighteen, he's been through rehab three times, you're his only hope."

"I'm his only hope?" Lo's low rumbling voice asked.

"Ok you're right, you're my only hope. Please,"

"Needles," Lo waved me into the room from where I was leaning against the door frame. "Did you look over that file I gave you yesterday?"

"The kid? Yeah, heroin, on the streets, in and out of rehab but it doesn't stick." I said shrugging. I was guessing this was the woman's brother, only when I looked at her closely now she was no more than a girl. Even in her police uniform she looked impossibly young.

Her blonde hair was pulled severely in a tight bun at the base of her skull and everything about her appearance said pressed and perfect. Her side arm was holstered and secured and all the gadgets that went on her belt were firmly in place.

"What did you think? You think he can be rehabbed?"

I shrugged, "Most people can be but they have to want to be. From the sounds of it this could be his last chance. It's rehab or death."

"What exactly do you know about it?" The girl demanded scowl-

5

ing at me. Slowly I started to undo the buttons of my long sleeved shirt. Most people didn't like to be told things, they wanted proof. "What –"

Before she could finish her question I had my shirt off and was holding out my arms to her. For the most part, both of my arms were covered in full sleeve tattoos, except for the insides of my elbows where track marks and scars stretched over my skin. I could have covered them with tattoos like I did the scar across my chest but these I needed to keep as a reminder. The girl closed her eyes and swallowed hard.

"I'm sorry, I was rude and you obviously know a lot about it." She whispered, not making eye contact.

"Needles?" Lo asked again. I nodded to him without taking my eyes off the girl. "Ok, this is Siobhan MacDonald, I'll leave you the office and you can get the information you need for her brother."

Siobhan

Fuck, I was so stupid. Hadn't I learned not to stick my foot in my mouth yet? What the hell was wrong with me?

"Look, I -," I started once Mr. Winters was gone.

"Stop," this new man named Needles said holding up a hand and then putting his shirt back on. "Just tell me about your brother."

"His name is Lachlan, we were actually born in Scotland but our parents moved here right after Lachy was born. Look, I'm really sorry about earlier," I sighed knowing that a positive relationship with the guy helping my brother get clean was important.

"Don't worry about it." Needles said buttoning his shirt up again. "Where is your brother now?"

"Jail, he's detoxing. He kind of went off the rails and got arrested and because I'm a cop I was called first. I set him up in a cell on the ok of my detachment commander is allowing me to keep him in the cell for a week but I know I'll have to move him to the hospital sooner rather than later."

"How many times has he detoxed?"

"Fully? Probably twice. Two of the times he's been in rehab he was kicked out and ended up back on the streets shooting up so he didn't get completely clean."

"So he knows that detoxing is the worst experience of his life and the only way to make the pain stop is to shoot up again. He needs to be mostly clean before he can come here." Needles said sitting on the couch on the far wall of the office. "Sit down please, I was up late last night and tilting my neck to look up at you is giving me a headache."

"Sorry," I said perching on the edge of a chair.

"Where are your parents? Why are you dealing with all of this?" he asked, rubbing his hands over his eyes.

"They've gone back to Scotland. They were told they were enabling Lachy and they needed to get some distance. They thought an entire ocean between them was the distance they needed." I muttered still not impressed to be the one stuck with Lachy. I would do everything I could to help him but I was still resentful and I could admit it.

"You going to work?" Needles asked, nodding at my uniform.

"No, just got off shift."

"Alright look, I'm not a counsellor or a therapist, I won't even be working with your brother all that much. My whole purpose here at the center is to watch the guys here and make sure they're not using. We have a no tolerance policy so if your brother, Lachlan is caught using anything he's out."

I nodded, completely agreeing with Needles' terms, anything to get my brother in here.

"You're nodding and agreeing but really it's your brother who has to agree and live by the rules. Will he do that?"

I sighed knowing Needles was right. "I don't know, honestly. When he's high he says he wants to get clean and not live like that anymore but of course when he's detoxing he's swearing at me and threatening to kill me if I don't get him a fix."

Needles nodded like he knew exactly what I was talking about and really he probably did.

"Lo said you're a tattoo artist, but that's not how you got your name is it?"

He watched me for a long time before he answered. "No."

"Um, could I ask you what your real name is? I'm having a hard time referring to you as Needles."

"You can ask," Needles said as he stood and walked to the door. "Your brother is expected here next Monday, that gives you a week to get him as clean as you can. He won't be treated well here. The other guys will consider him weak and pathetic and they will make sure he knows it. As far as they're concerned having never seen what they have in war he has no reason to be an addict. You won't be able to visit him, you can't call him or text him and you won't even be allowed on the compound grounds."

"For how long?"

"The foreseeable future."

"Will I get updates on his progress?"

"I can try but I can't promise you anything. I live here at the compound so I can keep an eye on your brother for you but I'm busy outside of here so don't expect a whole lot of information."

"I understand. Can I contact you if I have questions, or if I haven't heard from you for a while . . . if I don't do it too often?"

He smirked at me and turned and walked away calling back over his shoulder, "You can try!"

"You didn't tell me your name!" I called to him as another younger guy showed me to the main door of the clubhouse.

"I said you could ask, I never said I would tell you." And then he was gone and the door of the clubhouse was closed in my face.

Just freaking awesome, this was my last hope for my brother, a motorcycle club full of veterans. God I hoped this worked; this was Lachy's last chance, after this he was dead.

CHAPTER 2

Siobhan

I was sitting in front of the cell my brother was sleeping in. He was moaning and rolling around on the bed in pain. I knew withdrawal was bad but that didn't make it any easier watching it. I had left the MC clubhouse and gone home to shower and change and then had come straight back to the station.

I had to move Lachy to the hospital but I wasn't sure how I was going to do it on my own. Lachy wasn't huge but he was bigger than me and as strong as I was I couldn't move him if he didn't want to be moved.

I didn't have a lot of friends here so it's not like I had a huge list of people I could call for help. There was my douche ex-boyfriend and that was definitely out of the question and that was the end of my list.

My commander said I wasn't allowed to use any detachment resources to help my brother and I took that to mean man power as well. I jumped when I heard someone behind me clearing their throat.

I spun around to find Needles standing at the end of the row of empty cells.

"You scared me to death." I gasped with my hand holding my heart in my chest. "What are you doing here?"

Before he answered he walked all the way up the row and stood beside me watching my brother. His hands were in the pockets of his black jeans and he was wearing another long sleeved button up shirt.

"Guess I came to meet the patient." He replied shrugging.

"Well, here he is, Needles meet Lachy, Lachy this is Needles," I motioned to Lachy shivering on the cot. "He's asleep right now." Needles just nodded grimly.

"I was actually here to talk to one of the parole officers and re-membered you saying Lachlan was here. Are you moving him to the hospital?"

"Yeah," I sighed. "Then I remembered he outweighs me by more than fifty pounds when I've got all my gear on and he's not exactly helpful right now. I was trying to figure out how I was going to get him out of here."

"I'll help," Needles said, shrugging. "I'm here anyway. That is as long as you need the help."

"Yeah, Needles that would be really great, thank you." I said al-most gushing, how embarrassing, as I touched his arm. "I'll just go get the keys to the cell." I rushed away but not before I saw him staring at his arm where my hand was. I wonder what that meant, does he not like to be touched, or was it something else?

I quickly rushed out to get the guard to unlock Lachy's cell but was stopped when I ran into a hard chest and was held up by hard hands on my upper arms.

"Shit!" I exclaimed.

"That happy to see me, eh," my ex's voice said above me. I could tell he was very happy to have caught me like this.

"No, excuse me." I tried to move around him but he held me fast and I couldn't even move my feet. "Dean, let me go, I don't have time for this."

"Too bad," Dean said, smirking down at me. "What are you doing back here?"

"None of your business," I fired back at him and tried again to pull myself free.

"Wrong, you are very much my business." He said, shaking me a little. I was just pulling my knee back and aiming for his crotch when another voice behind me spoke up.

"She said to let her go." Needles said his voice hard.

"Fuck off Needles, what the fuck are you doing here anyway?" Dean demanded still holding my arms. "Shouldn't you be out pulling some dumb fuck out of a gutter?"

"Do it," was all Needles said and I let loose with my knee, connecting sharply with Dean's crotch. He didn't make that 'O' face that so many guys do but it was still comical how he turned bright red and he slumped to the floor. "Go get the guard and the keys."

I stepped over Dean and rushed to go get the guard to open Lachy's cell. I was only gone for a few minutes but when I got back Needles was standing from where he was crouching over Dean talking to him. I gave Needles a frown but he just shook his head.

"What the hell happened here?" The guard demanded when he saw Dean on the floor.

"Uh, he grabbed my arm and I didn't know he was there, reflex kick," I said shrugging as Needles laughed quietly behind the guard's back, who just harrumphed and led us back down the row of cells to Lachy's.

"Takin' this one to detox?" the guard asked as he unlocked Lachy's cell.

"Uh, yeah eventually, he's going to the War Angel's center." I said nodding. "I've gotta get him to the hospital though and get him clean first."

"I've heard good things about them, War Angels." The guard responded and waited in the hall while Needles lifted Lachy off the bed and over his shoulder.

Needles

Siobhan wasn't wrong, this kid was heavy and there was no way she could lift him on her own. If he outweighed her by fifty pounds when she was wearing all her gear then he had to be around two hundred pounds and it didn't help that at the moment he was dead weight. I was tall, but this fucker had to be close to Seether's height. It made me wonder how he got so tall and she was like a sprite, short and curvy.

"Stop it!" I scolded myself as I walked behind Siobhan with her brother over my shoulder.

"What?" she asked, turning back to me.

"Uh, nothing, your brother was um, twitching, made him hard to carry." I said thinking quickly. Couldn't have the girl think I was walking behind her watching her ass sway as she walked. She gave me a strange look but kept walking. She stopped beside a small sedan and opened the back door and I laid her brother on the back seat. "I've got my bike, I'll follow you to the hospital and help you unload him and get him checked in if you want."

"Oh, that would seriously be really amazing." She gushed, her face flushing with colour. I didn't really look closely at her earlier when she was in Lo's office and the light in the jail block sucked, but out here with the sun glinting off her blonde hair and her green eyes flashing I couldn't help but notice how beautiful she was. Yes she was short but she had curves everywhere they should be and where there weren't curves she was trim and looked to be packed with muscle.

"Uh, ok, I'll meet you there." And I did - meet Siobhan at the hospital. We got her brother checked in and all his paperwork filled out and she seemed to heave a sigh of relief as Lachlan was taken away on a gurney. She wouldn't see him again for a while because as soon as he was detoxed enough to leave the hospital he would be going to the War Angels center.

"Can I buy you a coffee?" She asked suddenly as we stepped out of the main doors. "I mean, if you drink coffee, or could I buy you a tea, I don't know, what do bikers drink?"

"Mostly beer," I chuckled, "But a coffee would be good."

"There's a coffee shop just across the street, how about that? We could walk."

"Sure," I said, shrugging. I was still wearing my leather bike jacket and she shoved her hands into the sweater she was wearing. It was nearing the end of September and it didn't look like we were going to get the same mild winter as last year. We entered the café and sat at a table by the window and when the waitress came by ordered coffee.

"So," She said when the waitress left. Siobhan wrapped her hands around her steaming cup and looked just about everywhere but at me.

"So," I said, taking a sip of my black coffee. "Why did you decide to become a cop?"

"Oh, I don't know," She said shrugging. "I just always thought it would be a great job. It's fun, it's exciting and challenging."

"You just wanted to carry a gun right?" I asked her, smirking. She snorted and laughed out loud shaking her head.

"Actually the gun is my least favourite part, but it's part of the job that I love so I carry it." She shrugged, smiling. "Why tattoos?"

"Well, I've always liked drawing ever since I was a kid and when I turned eighteen me and a bunch of guys dared each other to get one but let the person doing the tat to pick it. Luckily I got a hot chick doing mine and I convinced her to go easy on me." I shook my head remembering that day with those guys that a week later

I would never see again. "Turns out I have an addictive personality and ended up covering most of my torso with tats and to pay for my habit I started doing them for myself and others."

"What was that first one you got? Can I see it?"

"Ah, well that girl went easy on what she did for me but not where she put it. It's a little bull on my ass, so no you can't see it." I chuckled, shaking my head. Siobhan laughed at that then got serious.

"So, tattooing isn't how you got your name, does that have something to do with the marks on your arms?" She asked quietly, slowly tracing the rim of her coffee cup with her finger tip.

"Yup," I said nodding slowly. It's not like I had trouble talking about my past or how it came to be, I believed in being very open about that sort of thing and that being open would help me stay clean, but it seemed a little strange to be discussing it with her now.

"My brother's going to have track marks isn't he?" Tears were gathering in her eyes and she quickly wiped them away.

"I would think so. You said he's been using for a year, that's long enough for him to have developed them."

"How long have you been clean?"

"I took my last hit when I was twenty-one, that was four years ago." She nodded, fiddling with sugar packets. "Your brother's chances of getting clean are good. The hard part is staying clean. There's a lot going against him to stay clean that makes it hard. He needs a lot of support."

"How do you stay clean?" She asked me, raising her damp gaze to mine.

"One second at a time." I said quietly but earnestly. And it was true. "Good days you could do one at a time, but bad days it was one second at a time."

"Do you still have bad days?"

"More than I would like to admit. Being a recovering addict is not easy. The thing that made you an addict is still there, that shit doesn't go away but now I get to deal with that and the recovery, the cravings, the insomnia, guilt, shame. Sometimes I can be in the middle of a conversation and my thought processes just go sideways and I can't make sense of the simplest things. Sometimes I wake up in the morning after a particularly vivid nightmare and all I can think about is that next fix. That's the worst."

"How do you get to be so strong?"

I snorted and shook my head. "I don't think I'm strong, if I was strong I wouldn't have taken that first hit. If I was strong I could have stopped what had fucked me up to begin with."

"How can you say that? Did you cause that thing to happen?"

"No, I didn't cause it but that doesn't change the guilt."

"How did you get clean?"

"Lo found me on East Hastings, completely strung out. My parents had heard about the MC and what they were doing for vets. They asked him to find me and see if the MC could help me. I didn't want help at first but two nights later my best friend od'd sitting right beside me."

"I'm sorry," She whispered as a tear traced its way down her cheek.

"Don't be, at first I was just mad that he'd injected more than half of the heroin in the needle. And then he died, just like that," I snapped my fingers. "The next day I tracked Lo down at his hotel and begged him to help me."

"You've been with the MC ever since?"

I snorted at that, "Yeah, I've done some strange shit in the last four years."

"Like what?" she asked, finally smiling.

"Your smile is amazing." I said quietly then watched her blush and clear her throat. "One of the brothers, Hammer, got Axle the VPs sister pregnant and she wanted a special way to tell him so she asked me to draw a baby on her belly, like with the cord and everything. Apparently it went over well 'cause they had triplets and are getting married in the summer."

"What else?" she asked, chuckling.

"Lo's wife Alana is also an artist and sometimes she designs tats for people. After meeting Lo she designed one for him of a soldier kneeling with his head bowed holding dog tags and huge beat up angel wings over him. Lo had me put it on his back and never in my life have I been afraid of fucking up a tattoo 'cause I couldn't see through my own tears." I shook my head and smiled slightly at the memory.

Siobhan and I talked for at least another hour, about nothing and everything and then she looked at her watch and said she had to get going. She was working that night and had to get some sleep. I tossed a twenty on the table even though our coffee couldn't have cost more than six dollars with free refills but what the hell; we'd sat at that table a long time.

When we got back to her car we exchanged numbers and I promised her when her brother got to the MCs center I would let her know and I would keep her up to date as much as I could. She squinted up at me and smiled then stretched up on her toes and kissed my cheek before she got in her car and drove away.

CHAPTER 3

Siobhan

"You know that little trick of yours won't be forgotten any time soon." Dean said as he sat on the edge of my desk in the station a week after checking my brother into the hospital. I was just finishing a report on a domestic violence case I had pulled today and then I was clocking out for three whole days. I hadn't heard from Needles yet about whether or not they had gotten Lachy to the center.

"I have no idea what you're talking about Dean." I muttered as I typed the last few sentences then jumped and yelped when Dean slammed his hand down on my keyboard.

"Yes you fucking do. You think you can kick me in the balls and get away with it? You better watch yourself Sha-vaughn," He threatened, stretching out my name. "You'll get yours." He whispered as he leaned close and licked the shell of my ear.

"Fuck I hate lawyers," I whispered to myself when I was sure he was gone.

"Only you and the rest of the world." My friend Casey said flopping into the chair beside my desk. "What did the douche do now?"

"Oh, nothing but words." I said shrugging it off.

"You and I both know that more often than not those words don't stay just words." Casey said pointing her half eaten Mars bar at me. "How's your brother?"

"Don't know," I shrugged. "I put him in the hospital a week ago and he should be going to the War Angel's center today but I haven't heard from my contact there."

"Well, that's not necessarily a bad thing." Casey shrugged and took a big bite of her chocolate bar.

"You've met Lachy right?"

"Only at his best," She joked and levered herself out of the chair. Casey and I were complete opposites, she was tall and thin, I was short and curvy, she ate only candy and chocolate, or so it seemed, and didn't gain a pound, I looked at a slice of pizza and gained ten pounds. She never worked out or exercised in any way shape or form and spent the majority of my free time working out. Casey had pixie short black hair that she spiked and coloured the tips of. Today they were green. "You headed out?"

"Yeah, you?" I replied as I shut down my computer.

"Nah, just getting here." She said, shaking her head. "How the hell did we get on completely opposite shifts?"

"Luck of the draw?" I shrugged.

"I bet the douche had something to do with it." She said, her eyes narrowing dangerously.

"I highly doubt that." I said, chuckling and shaking my head.

"Yeah, you're probably right. I better get up to dispatch before the dragon lady decides I'm late." Casey turned her long stride down the hall in the opposite direction I was going. "Talk at ya later bitch!"

I shook my head as I watched her go and chuckled to myself, then pulled my phone out of my pocket and checked for messages from Needles for about the millionth time that day. I sighed and tipped my head back then straightened my shoulders and went to shower and change to head home.

Needles

"I thought you'd be blowing up my phone by now." I said from where I was leaning against my bike in Siobhan's driveway.

"Needles! What are you doing here?" she demanded as she stepped out of her car. "How'd you know where I lived? My address is unlisted."

"I have my own personal geek squad." I shrugged knowing Seether would find that funny instead of insulting and so would his fiancé Grace-Lynn AKA Pixie.

"Huh, if I hadn't been begging the iPhone gods for a text from you all day I would say that's incredibly illegal and possibly write you a fine."

"Is that so? The iPhone gods eh?"

"Eh," she shrugged, "So, why did you hunt me down?"

"I wanted to give you an update on your brother."

"You could have texted me that."

"True, but I couldn't see your beautiful smile through a text."

"You could've asked for a picture."

"I could've, would you have sent me a picture?"

"Never hurts to ask . . . but no, probably not." She said wrinkling her nose. "Do you want to continue this conversation in the driveway or would you rather come in?"

"Um, in I guess."

"You guess? If the answer's no then just say no."

I shook my head, "The answer is definitely yes, but I'm afraid that once I get into your house there won't be a lot of talking about your brother."

"Oh, what will we be talking about?" She asked, her eyebrows shooting into her hairline. I had been slowly walking towards her the entire time we talked and now I stood so close I could feel her breath on my throat above my t-shirt.

"This," I replied and sealed my lips over hers then after just a moment I pulled back and said, "And how I shouldn't want to do that and shouldn't do it again, but I do want that and I will do it over and over again."

"Why shouldn't you?" she asked peering up at me through her eyelashes.

"Because I'm working with your brother."

"Are you his doctor?"

"No."

"Counselor, or therapist?"

"No."

"Then is there really a conflict of interest?"

"Probably."

"Come inside I'll make you supper while you tell me about Lachy." She took my hand and led me into the house.

CHAPTER 4

Siobhan

"I have to warn you, now that I've invited you in for supper that I'm not that great a cook." I said dropping my bag just inside the door and pulling my side arm from it then walking down the hall to my bedroom to lock my gun up. "Sorry, had to put it away." I said when I stepped back into the living room.

Needles was there looking at the pictures I had hanging on my wall. Most of them were of Lachy and me with a few of our parents scattered through. Some were even taken on our last trip to Scotland before Lachy started using. He turned when I came back into the room and smiled slightly.

"Ok, seriously I can't keep calling you Needles, please tell me what your name is?" I begged, my shoulder slumping.

He chuckled and shook his head. "What bothers you about my name? What it is or what it means?"

"It's meaning doesn't bother me." I said shaking my head, absolutely 100% honestly. "I understand what it means and where it came from and that doesn't bother me. Your addiction doesn't bother me; it worries me yes because I know relapse could be just around the corner. It's really not about the name at all so much as it is me. It just makes me feel silly to call you Needles."

He watched me seriously for a minute. He stared for so long I started to worry that I had insulted him.

"Never mind, I'll –"

"Jaxon," He said quietly. "My name is Jaxon." I blinked at him, not sure I had heard him correctly and then realizing what he was trusting me with I smiled.

"Thank you." Instead of making a big deal of it and embarrassing us each more I turned and hurried into the kitchen, which of course in my tiny house was three steps away from the living room with only a table separating them. "So, what can I microwave for you?"

"Seriously?" He chuckled, apparently shocked at my lack of culinary skills.

"What? You talk, I'll nuke, tell me about my brother, is he at the clubhouse?"

"Yeah, he made it over to the center. He was a little worse for wear but he made it."

"What does that mean?" I asked skeptically.

"Well, he chose to put up a fight when we picked him up. He accidently threw a punch at Axle's fiancé and pissed him off so he punched your brother."

"Why was Axle's fiancé there?"

"She's our resident psychologist, or she will be, she's still working on her Masters."

"Oh, is she ok?" I asked opening my freezer to see what not so delicious dish I could warm up for Jaxon.

"Oh yeah, she'll have a bit of a bruise, but she'll be more angry when Axle doesn't let her do anything for a few weeks because she's pregnant again."

"Oh my God! My brother punched a pregnant woman?" I demanded in shock.

"Well yeah but it was an accident, he was aiming at Axle."

"This calls for real food, let's go, I'm taking you out for supper. I need some carbs."

Needles

"You know, most people in a difficult situation say they need a drink, not carbs." I said sitting in the passenger seat of her car as we drove through town.

"And so would I say I needed a drink if I actually drank. Carbs are my guilty pleasure." She said signalling to turn at a light.

"Where are we going?"

"Pizza." She muttered parallel parking the car.

"We just passed three Boston Pizza's and four Pizza Hut's."

"That's sacrilege." Siobhan spat as she got out of the car. I followed her out and stood on the sidewalk in front of a little place that I had never heard of before. "There is no better pizza than Bold Pizzeria."

I followed Siobhan as she pulled open the front door and stepped inside. The place was relatively busy for a Monday night but there were a couple of empty tables. Instead of waiting to be seated she immediately went to the back corner and sat at a small booth. I sat across from her, noticing that she sat so she could see the door, putting my back to it.

"Hey Vaughn!" I turned at the chipper voice that had bounced over to our table to find a young girl who couldn't be legal, wearing a half apron and carrying a glass of dark carbonated liquid. "Diet Coke, no ice, how've you been?"

"Pretty good, busy you?"

"Same old, I'm almost finished my GED course, now I just have to take the test and I can be done with school for a little while."

"That's great Chrissy, how's little Ben?"

"Oh he's so great, he started crawling the little stinker! Now he's into everything!"

"That's great, can you get my friend a beer?" She asked, pointing to me.

"Oh no, just a Coke is fine." I said holding my hands up.

"You sure? We've got some pretty good domestic stuff." Chrissy said, then laughed and eyed Siobhan, "Or so I've been told!"

"I sure hope so! You have another year to go before you're allowed to drink!" Siobhan laughed at the girl. "I'll have my usual but can you bring a menu out?"

"You betcha!" and Chrissy turned and left the table.

"You didn't want a beer?" Siobhan asked me curiously.

"Recovering addict," I said pointing to my own chest, "I try not to consume anything that could cause me to relapse." She smiled and nodded then waited as I read the menu that Chrissy dropped off with my Coke. "Ok, so tell me what I should order, you obviously come here a lot."

"I always get the same thing so I'm not really the best person to ask." She said, shaking her head.

"What do you get?"

"Chicken, bacon, mushrooms and cheese." She said, shrugging. "I usually tell anyone I bring here to order what they would normally order from anywhere else and then be prepared for a life changing experience."

"Ok," I said closing my menu just as Chrissy came back over. "Vegetarian please."

"Vegan and gluten free?" Chrissy asked.

"No, real cheese please and a regular crust." I replied surprised vegan and gluten free were options.

"Ok, be right back."

"Really? Vegetarian?" Siobhan asked with a strange look on her face.

"Really, I don't eat much meat, definitely not pork or beef."

"Is that part of your recovery?"

"No, it's part of what made me an addict to begin with." I answered really not wanting to get into this conversation over dinner. "I promise to tell you about it some time, just not now. It's not an easy discussion and during supper is a really bad time for it."

"Ok, but you don't need to feel obligated to tell me." She said sitting back against the booth.

"I don't feel obligated. I don't know why I want to tell you things. I really shouldn't spend much time with you at all but I feel drawn to you. There's something about you that makes me want to be with you."

"I find that kind of curious given how we met and how rude I was to you." She said tilting her head to the side.

"You weren't rude, you were upset and you didn't know who I was. As far as you knew I was just some guy off the street called in to judge your brother. I didn't take it personally then and I don't hold it against you now."

"Hmm, that's good." She sipped her drink then looked my right in the eye. "So you said earlier at the house we were going to talk about that kiss."

"Yeah, we should talk about that, but I'd rather just repeat it." I said nodding but not making any other movement.

"I would also like to repeat it but I don't want repeating it to make you uncomfortable. I like you Jaxon, and as much as I want to be your friend or possibly more my brother's recovery is most important to me. So if you tell me that you can't have a relationship with me past a few text updates and still help my brother then that's what this will be."

I watched her and I could see the trepidation in her eyes. She had totally just laid it all bare for me and I could take the out and totally back off but I didn't think she wanted that any more than I did. I wanted to tell her that I could only text her once in a while but I knew that would be a lie. I knew I would text her and it would be to meet for coffee to talk about her brother. Then I would tell her one thing about her brother and talk for hours about her. I was just about to tell her that when Chrissy came back with our food.

"Here you go guys," The girl said, placing a tray on the table. "It's still hot so be careful." On the tray were two slightly bigger than personal sized pizzas. They smelled and looked amazing.

"Thanks Chrissy," Siobhan said smiling at the girl. We didn't talk much for the rest of the meal except to ask each other if the food was good. She insisted on paying for the pizza and I had to admit by the time we were finished I had just had a religious experience, best pizza ever.

We drove back to Siobhan's place in silence as well. As soon as she got into the car she turned the radio on and Creed blasted through the speakers. I was starting to get the feeling that she took my silence to mean that I wasn't able to be more than what her brother needed. She was so wrong and she would find that out soon enough.

She parked in her driveway and turned the car off, staring out the windshield. Then she took a deep breath and turned to me with her hand outstretched.

"Well –"

Before she could finish I cupped her cheeks in each of my hands and sealed my mouth over hers, licking her lips and tasting her pizza and her Diet Coke and her and once again I was addicted.

Siobhan gasped and I licked inside her mouth and sucked her tongue back into my mouth and we dueled until I had to pull back to take a breath. I nipped and sucked at her lips and then kissed her hard again.

"I'll see you tomorrow," I said and turned and climbed out of the car.

CHAPTER 5

Needles

I had the early shift at the tattoo shop this morning and I always showed up early to double check the till and the receipts from the night before. It wasn't that I didn't trust my staff, I just like to be sure. I was just putting it all away when my new guy walked in the front door.

Lix was one of the first guys to go through and finish at the War Angel's new center. Before we all stayed at the farm house that Lo and his wife Alana and their family lived in.

Lix, short for Felix which he hated, had done a short stint in the armed forces but saw more than enough to give any guy PTSD. He hadn't sunk into addiction but he had been in a Humvee that had driven over an IED and while he had walked away he had completely lost his hearing.

"Hey man," I said holding my fist out for a bump. Lix was a super talented artist and I was lucky to have him working at the store. Most of his suffering didn't come from what he saw overseas or what he did or really anything war related. His suffering came from the constant ringing in his ears after the blast.

"Hey," thankfully he could still speak though sometimes he needed to be reminded not to yell, and he knew sign language. We had all learned at least a little bit of sign language when Hammer came out because he couldn't talk for awhile due to an injury after an IED went off under his Humvee.

"What's on the schedule for the day?" Lix asked looking down at the appointment book. I knew better than to talk to him when he wasn't looking at me so I just waited until he looked back up. "Says here Ashlyn Cameron? Is that Pixie's sister?"

"I think so." I said shrugging.

"Huh, it says here it's just a consult," Lix said looking down at the book again. He sometimes forgot that he couldn't hear and that we couldn't communicate with him unless he was looking at us. "With you or me?"

"If you want it you can have it," I said when he looked at me again.

"What?" We were still working on lip reading.

If you want the appointment it's yours. Doesn't matter to me, I signed and shrugged again. Lix just nodded then headed back to the smaller rooms we used for tattooing. We tried to give our clients as much privacy as possible even though our rooms had no doors. I also tried to make sure each of our artists had their own space and no one messed with anyone else's space.

Not all of my employees were vets or members of War Angel's but the guys who showed an interest in art and tattooing who came through the clubhouse got a second look from me.

I was looking for more women in the shop but so far none had come in looking for a job, just some ink. So far our appointment book wasn't very full and Ashlyn was our first appointment scheduled and she wouldn't be here for another hour.

My first appointment wasn't for another two hours so I thought this would be a good time to do some inventory. I was in the back room when Pixie found me.

"Hey," She said, knocking on the door frame. "Are you the only one here?"

"No, Lix is here, he's the one who's supposed to be working with Ashlyn today." I said walking with Pixie back to the front. "Didn't he ... shit, I forgot to turn on the flasher."

"The flasher?"

"Yeah, Lix is deaf; he probably didn't hear the bell on the door. We had a system installed that makes the lights flash if he's the only one up here, sorry Pixie."

"That's ok," She said shrugging. "We purposely had nothing planned today. Besides," She said stopping just past the entrance to the hall, "It looks like Ashlyn found Lix."

I stepped out from behind her to see Lix and Ashlyn smiling at each other and laughing at the front counter. She was writing notes, answering his questions about the tattoo she wanted and he was talking just a little too loudly. She apparently thought it was cute because she kept giggling.

"I guess you're in good hands." I said smiling and turned back to the store room.

"Thanks Needles." Pixie called as she walked back around the front counter to her sister.

The rest of the day went pretty quickly. After my first appointment we ended up having enough walk in business to keep Lix and I and two other artists busy for the rest of the day. We barely got time to have a coffee break in between customers. Finally we were closing up and Lix and I were alone in the shop.

"Did you know Ashlyn's an artist?" He called to me even though I was only two feet away from him. I shook my head no as he kept talking about the young girl from earlier this morning. "She designed her tat, it's really well done. If you're still looking for women to work here you should tap her. She'd probably be really good."

I tapped him on the shoulder to get his attention then signed, *What's your interest in this girl? You know she's not legal yet right?*

"Yeah I know, she's hot but I'm not stupid. I can wait a year or so." He replied, shaking his head. "I'm only twenty, not like there's a huge age difference, but yeah, I'll wait."

"Good," I said and nodded.

Siobhan

Jaxon had said I'll see you tomorrow before he got out of the car last night. Did that mean he was going to call? Did that mean he was just going to show up on my doorstep again?

Damn I was so confused. This was ridiculous. And then my phone chimed. It was the tone I had given Needles and I just about jumped out of my skin.

I looked at my phone and saw a text:

**Got caught up at work before I stopped
at the clubhouse to see your brother,
on my way over if that's ok. 15?**

Oh geez, he was on his way over now. Well, he didn't just stop by; he gave me a little warning at least. A whole fifteen minutes. Shit!

That ok?

Oh shit, he wanted an answer.

**Yeah, that's great I'm just going to jump in the shower
so I'll leave the door open for you.**

Don do that I'll wait outside til u'r finished in shower.

It's ok really it's only 15 min

No its not safe don leave door unlocked I can wait.

Ok

I thought that was odd, but I wasn't going to argue with him about it. I tried to be in and out of the shower quickly but still by the time I got out and dressed again Jaxon was sitting on my front step.

"Sorry, have you been waiting long?" I asked as I opened the door.

"Nope, just got here," He said standing and stepping towards me. He slipped his hands around my waist and held me still as he leaned in and kissed me lightly but passionately.

"Come on in." I took his hand and pulled him inside to the couch then went to the fridge to get him a Coke and me a Diet Coke. "So, your first text said you were busy at work?"

"Yeah, not so much this morning but after lunch we had a lot of walkins." He sounded cranky about that.

"Is that bad?"

"No, business is business it's just people who walk into a tattoo parlor instead of making an appointment are usually less serious about the tattoo and more wishy washy about what they want. They have trouble making a decision and hold up the rest of the shop."

"Do you guys work on commission?" I asked, totally ignorant about the whole process. Jaxon rested his head on the back of the couch then reached over and started playing with a strand of my hair.

"Yes and no, it's always nice to get more paying customers in but if the guys do a shit job and the customer complains then we lose business and customers. The guys get credit for the number of customers they see but they also get credit on customer reviews."

"That's cool," I said scooting closer to him and resting my bent knees on his thigh.

"What did you do today? Did you work?"

"Nope, I was off today and again tomorrow. Mostly today I just hung out and cleaned the house. Talked to my parents on skype, got some groceries that didn't go in my freezer." I chuckled, remembering last night trying to make him supper.

"That's good. I saw your brother today. He's still detoxing but not as bad. He's refusing to get out of bed which is fine for now, he's not using and that's a step in the right direction."

"I bet he's miserable." I sighed, shaking my head. "Sorry about that."

"Nothing for you to be sorry about," Jaxon said, shrugging. "That's on him and he'll get away with it for a little while longer but eventually Brooke will have him up and helping."

We were silent for a few minutes as he continued to play with my hair and I watched his face. He had very little expression except for his eyes. His eyes were a deep chocolate brown that I could easily dive into.

They were ringed with the longest blackest eyelashes I had ever seen, women killed for those kinds of lashes. Mascara companies promised those kinds of lashes. Jaxon's jaw was strong and his nose straight but his eyes made him gorgeous.

"Your hair is like silk," he murmured, burying his hand in it and pulling me closer to him. I went willingly and paused just before my lips landed on his. "I should tell you something."

"Ok," I whispered, "Should I be worried?"

"I don't think so," He said, frowning slightly. "I haven't been with anyone in a few years."

"Ok, neither have I." I said, shrugging then leaning forward and kissing him. Is this when I told him I had only been with one person ever and I really didn't enjoy it?

"I was always worried about the needles, they weren't always clean. I never did anything . . . um, to get my fix but I shared needles with a guy who did. I've been tested and I'm clean, I get tested every three months just to be sure, but I wanted you to know."

Jaxon had cupped my jaw with his palm while the other hand stayed anchored in my hair as he talked. This was very important for him to tell me, I could see it in his eyes and I knew I couldn't trivialize it by keeping my secret.

"Thank you for telling me, I know that was important and not easy for you." I whispered and kissed his lips lightly again. "I . . . only ever . . . with one person." I said, stumbling over my words.

"Oh wow," he whispered, his eyes wide. "Are you thinking of . . . with me?"

"Maybe, are you thinking of it with me?"

"Fuck yes."

Oh, ok, good." I murmured, staring deeply into his eyes.

He smirked at me then said, "Yeah, good. But not tonight, I can wait."

"Oh," I said, frowning. "Will you kiss me though?"

"Fuck yes," he murmured again and pulled me to him again kissing me like he was lost in the desert and I was the first drink of water he'd had in weeks.

CHAPTER 6

Needles

Today was Saturday and I was not working at the tattoo parlor. I was instead at the center trying to get Lachlan out of the barracks. He had been at War Angel's for just about a week and he had yet to get out of bed for anything but food.

Not that he ate much anyway, the rest of the guys, there were five others, ate mostly everything before he got to the table we were using as a buffet. Right now he was refusing to get out of bed for even food and I had tried to convince him he needed to get up and start his recovery but it was no good. He kept demanding to see his sister and no amount of bribing him would get him moving.

As I stepped outside Brooke was on her way in. Her baby, Imogen was eight months old and I'm pretty sure I heard her tell Alana that Axle was trying to get her pregnant again.

As she walked past me she winked and put her finger to her lips, shushing me. I heard nothing for a few minutes until she yelped. I was about to go back inside when she started talking.

"Well, I didn't think anyone was in here." She exclaimed. I heard Lachlan mumble something but it wasn't clear enough to understand.

"No, no good cop. Was Needles being the bad cop? That's funny. No, I just came in here to get some sleep without my fiancé trying to get me pregnant." She said and it sounded like she was trying to get comfortable. "I figured right now the barracks would be empty and quiet. Don't mind me, you go ahead and do whatever you need."

Lachlan mumbled something else and there was more rustling of blankets and squeaking of cot springs. Brooke seemed to ignore him and started humming, a church hymn, Amazing Grace I think.

"Isn't that a beautiful hymn?" I heard her say, and Lachlan reply. "Oh, I wasn't talking to you." Brooke said then Lachlan's rumbling question. "Well, I was talking to God of course. Don't you talk to God when you're alone?"

"Fuck," Lachlan exclaimed, that was clear enough.

"Don't mind me," Brooke said cheerfully, "God and I have these little talks all the time. Of course usually there isn't anyone else in the room but I highly doubt God will mind if you listen in."

"I'm not fucking listening!" Lachlan yelled at her and his cot springs squeaked again.

"Oh, ok then, I'll just pretend you're not there then. I mean, this room was supposed to be empty so really I am well within my rights to talk to God."

"Whatever," Lachlan muttered.

"God what should I do?" Brooke asked the air, or perhaps she really was talking to God. "David is determined to get me pregnant again. I have told him that I want to wait until A) we're married and B) Imogen is a little older, like at least a year, but he just won't listen. Every night he's on me like a rabid beast and I just can't say –"

"Enough!" Lachlan roared and stomped out of the barracks. He stopped when he saw me leaning against the wall and glared at me. "I don't care how many fucking horse stalls I have to clean out, don't make me listen to her fucking pray anymore!"

And then he was gone and Brooke was stepping out of the door beside me. I held my hand out palm up and she slapped it giving me five. Lachlan may never live this down, but then neither will Axle.

Siobhan

I was on my fourth of five days on shift and I was watching the clock. Ten hour shifts were normal and for the most part I enjoyed them but some days even a two hour shift would be hard. Three domestic violence calls in one day in three vastly different areas of the city and I was exhausted and disheartened. And let's not forget about the two hit and runs and the kids who broke into the liquor store at noon.

One more hour and then I could clock out and go home, run a hot bath and soak in it until the water was cold. That sounded like heaven. Maybe I would call Bold Pizzeria and order a pizza for pick up on my way home.

I was just about to call in my order when my radio went off, calling me to a single vehicle accident on the highway heading east towards Monte Creek, the same highway that the War Angel's clubhouse was off of.

I quickly grabbed my radio and replied to the call, "This is unit 6, I'm en route."

"Affirmative unit 6," the dispatcher came back, "We have reports of casualties, the bus is also en route, break-"

"Go ahead,"

"Unit 12 is also en route, two juvenile males and one juvenile female involved in the accident."

"Affirmative," I replied and turned on all my lights and sirens.

Six hours later I was stumbling into my house, pizza and bath forgotten. All I wanted now was sleep and lots of it. I had to be up again in ten hours and get back to the detachment for my next shift so really a hot bath and pizza would have to wait anyway. I quickly shot off a text to Jaxon letting him know I wasn't ignoring him and his earlier text.

Horrible day, having a quick shower, then to bed
TTYT

> **Sorry to hear ur day sucked**
> **Hope you get some sleep**
> **TTYS**

That done I jumped quickly into the shower, turning the water on as hot as I could handle and just stood under the spray for at least ten minutes before shutting it off. Then I wrapped a towel around me and dropped into bed only to dream about dead kids with severed limbs.

After parking my car in the garage below the detachment I rode the elevator up to the floor I worked on. There was a message there waiting for me saying I had a visitor in the lobby. I hurried back to the elevator and rode back down to the lobby. There I found Jaxon sitting off to the side but as soon as he saw me he walked over to me.

"Hey, what are you doing here?" I asked, hoping he wouldn't try to kiss me. It was really not professional to be kissing guys in my uniform.

"You said last night you had a tough day, I thought you could use some coffee this morning." He said smiling and handing over an extra-large cup from Tim Horton's.

"Oh wow! Thank you so much! I chose to sleep an extra fifteen minutes instead of stopping for coffee." I said taking the first sip. "Why didn't you just come by the house?"

"I knew you were working day shift today but not what time so I thought it was safer to catch you here." He said shrugging, his hands buried in his pockets again.

"This is heavenly!" I exclaimed, sipping the hot coffee again.

"Are you busy tonight? Can we hang out?"

"Sure, that would be great. I'm off at 5 barring any horrible accidents or something like that. I'm supposed to be on patrol in an hour though and I've got a ton of paperwork to do from yesterday."

"I heard about that accident yesterday, sorry you were there."

I shrugged and wrinkled my nose, "Part of the job."

"Well, I'll let you get to it then. Be safe today hey? I'll come by around seven?"

"Yeah, sure that sounds great." I nodded and stood watching him leave. He turned at the door and waved then disappeared.

"Who is that yumminess?" Casey asked sneaking up behind me. I didn't even turn to look at her; I just watched the door like a sad puppy.

"That was Jaxon, AKA Needles. He's with the War Angel's MC and is sort of working with my brother at their center helping with his rehab." I said smiling up at my friend.

"Wow," Casey said, staying to watch out the door as I turned back to the elevator. "So, when do I get to meet him? Where does he work? Does he really ride a motorcycle?" she asked rapid-fire as she turned to join me in the elevator.

"I don't know, he owns a tattoo parlor and yes." I answered each of her questions in turn.

"More importantly does he have any single friends?"

"Again, I don't know. I've only met one other guy at the MC and I know he's married. Jaxon's talked about other guys but always attached a woman's name. Like Lo's wife Alana or Axle's fiancé Brooke, that sort of thing." I replied shrugging.

"No one single?" Casey pouted.

"I don't think so," I chuckled at her sad face. "I'm sure the entire MC isn't married or attached, there have to be single guys in there somewhere."

"You gotta ask, do they have wild parties like on Sons of Anarchy?"

"I honestly don't know, and if they did I don't know that I could attend, you know from a legal standpoint."

"So you're ok dating one of the guys but not going to a party? You know, from a legal standpoint?"

"You know what I mean." I said rolling my eyes at her.

"Yeah I do, you on shift right now?"

"Yup, on till five, let's hope for a quieter day than yesterday."

CHAPTER 7

Needles

I stood at Siobhan's door with my fist raised to knock and hesitated. For the first time in a long time I wanted a relationship to work. I wanted to get to know Siobhan and have her be a part of my life and I was afraid that if her brother's rehab didn't stick neither would she. I took a deep breath and knocked on the door then waited.

When the door flew open I was greeted to some of the most amazing smells ever to greet my nose.

"You're just in time, come on in!" Siobhan exclaimed holding the door wide.

"What is that smell?" I asked, lifting my nose to the air again.

"Cullen Skink and Bridie pie," She replied and laughed at my face.

"What?"

"Haddock soup and beef pie," She chuckled, shaking her head. "I figured since you brought me that much needed and very much appreciated coffee this morning the least I could do was cook you supper. I don't usually cook for people because all I really know how to make are traditional Scottish dishes."

"So, no haggis?"

"Gross, no, I don't like haggis."

"Awesome!" I said as she closed the door then I grabbed her around the waist and pulled her into my. "I missed you." I said, cupping her cheek with my palm and lowering my mouth to hers.

She easily opened her mouth to my questing tongue and kissed me back just as deeply as I kissed her. I groaned as I pulled back from her just a little and kissed her a few more times lightly.

"I would like nothing more than to stand here and kiss you and hold you all night but I am starving." I whispered between each little peck. I kissed her hard one more time then pulled back and held her at arms-length. "Feed me woman!"

She giggled and took my hand, pulling me to her little kitchen table. "Sit down, I'll bring you your soup."

"What's that called again?"

"Cullen Skink," she replied, setting a bowl in front of me that smelled so good I swore I had started drooling.

"What does that mean?"

"It's like clam chowder but the haddock is smoked. The Cullen part is an area of Scotland." She replied, placing a plate of home-made rolls on the table between us.

"And the skink part?"

"That's the lower part of an animal leg, like the shin bone. They're usually boiled for soup so the word skink became known as soup."

"Wow, this is amazing." I said as I took another bite. "You can cook Scottish food for me anytime you like. What's a bridie pie?"

"It's a meat pie with either beef or lamb with onions and spices."

"You know a lot of Scottish history, or is that just something you know 'cause you were born there?"

"No, I definitely didn't know much about Scotland, I did quite a bit of research when I was a kid. Especially the first time we went back to visit."

"You came over when you were really young hey?"

"Yeah, I think about six, Lachy was a baby."

"I guess your parents still have pretty thick accents."

"Aye laddie, deh ya ken it!" She said, her accent so thick I just laughed. "Haud yer wheesht!" she exclaimed and laughed with me.

"What the hell did that mean?" I asked, still laughing.

"That last one? It meant hold your tongue or be quiet." She said giggling softly.

"Ok," I said when we had calmed down enough, "Why's it called a bridie pie?"

"It's either because they were served at most weddings or because they were invented by a playwright by the same name." She said smiling as she cut into one of her bridie pies and let the steam rise with the amazing aroma.

"God, that smells amazing!" I said cutting my own open and letting the scent take me over. We ate quietly for a while just enjoying the food. I had completely forgotten my apprehension from earlier standing outside her door, until I looked up to find her watching me with a smile on her face. "What?"

"Nothing," She said, shaking her head and smirking as she went back to eating.

"No really, what? What were you thinking?"

"Just something a friend said to me this morning."

"What was that?"

"It was just after you left the detachment this morning," She said and sighed then laughed again. "Casey wanted to know who the yumminess was."

"Me? Your friend thought I was yummy?"

"You are yummy." Siobhan said blushing and bit her bottom lip. "She wanted to know if there were other single guys in the MC."

"Oh yeah, lots but don't ask me who 'cause other than Lo, Axle, Seether and Hammer no one else even crosses my mind most days." I said shaking my head.

"Why those four?"

"You met Lo, he's the president. Axle is his VP and he and his fiancé just had a baby plus she's the counsellor at the center. Seether is our geek squad and his fiancé came to us under rather difficult circumstances. And Hammer and his fiancé who is Axle's sister just had triplets. The rest of the guys at the MC are acquaintances and like when we were all in the armed forces we've got each other's backs but those four are my . . . friends."

Siobhan

"That was difficult for you to say wasn't it? That those four men are your friends." I said tilting my head to the side.

"Yeah," He shrugged like it was no big deal but I knew it was.

"Why? Why those men?"

"Lo pulled me out of the gutter and where Lo goes Axle goes. They served together, they started the MC together, they've known each other almost their entire lives. You don't ever get one without the other." He said nodding as he talked.

He had finished his meal and had pushed his dishes away just a bit and sat back in his chair. I thought maybe he would feel more comfortable talking about this if I was busy clearing the table and not completely focused on him.

"And Seether?"

"He's the same age as me, we've been close because once I got clean he was the guy who knew the anger I felt. He experienced something very different than I did but felt the same guilt and anger. And Hammer is also a recovering addict but his drug of choice was oxy."

I put a plate of Scottish shortbread cookies in front of him and sat in my chair again.

"You baked cookies too?" he asked, smiling and taking one.

"Oh no, I've never been able to get them right, these are the closest I've found to the real thing though."

"I have to tell you what your brother did last week." He said, chuckling and shaking his head. "So . . ." he told me about Lachy refusing to get out of bed and Brooke going into the barracks to find somewhere quiet to rest since her fiancé kept trying to get her pregnant and wouldn't let her sleep at night. She started by humming Amazing Grace and then 'praying' to God to ask for guidance. By the time she got to Axle's beastliness Lachy was out of bed and shoveling out horse stalls and has been helping ever since.

I couldn't stop laughing. The things Jaxon said and the way he talked had me laughing so hard I almost fell off my chair. Finally we calmed enough that we could breathe without bursting out laughing again we stood and went to the couch in the living room. We fell against the cushions and he started playing with my hair again.

"I'm never going to be able to wear my hair up with you around." I joked, turning so I was facing him. He lifted my legs and draped them over his lap so he could move even closer to me.

"It's just so soft, I can't get over how it feels." He said almost reverently. "The colour is so beautiful the way it shines in the sun, you have so much of it, it must be heavy."

"I guess," I shrugged, "I've never really thought about it but I guess at the end of a long shift my neck is sore."

"Do you have a lot of bad days like yesterday?"

"No, yesterday was rare but at the same time that stuff happens all too often as well." I could feel him watching me as he played with my hair, his other hand resting on my thigh. I scooted closer to him so my butt touched his leg and my knees were bent against his chest and leaned forward, pressing my lips to his. As much as I loved his lips on mine this position was not a comfortable one so I moved so I was straddling his lap facing him and I could put my hands on him easier.

"I have more updates on your brother." He whispered as I slid my hands into his hair.

"I don't want my brother between us, it can wait." I said and some tension seemed to leave him before he levered up and kissed me, licking into my mouth, his hands on my hips flexing. Then his arms were around me and one hand was buried in my hair at the back of my head. "I don't want to wait for you any longer though."

"What does that mean?" he whispered looking up at me and brushing my hair off of my face.

"I want you to make love to me." I whispered back ducking in quickly to continue kissing him so I wouldn't see his eyes in case he was going to say no. He kissed me back passionately and then scooted to the edge of the couch and lifted me to stand.

"Are you sure?" He asked, breathing hard and holding my hips. I nodded and tried to kiss him again but he held me away. "I need the words Siobhan, I need you to say you are sure that you want me to make love to you tonight, that if we go any further right now it's because you want me."

"I do, I want you and I want this tonight, I want you to make love to me, I want to make love to you, I am sure." I said locking my gaze with his so he could see how serious I was. He nodded once

47

and kissed me then pushed me towards my bedroom.

CHAPTER 8

Needles

I couldn't believe what she had asked me, what she had told me. She wants me to make love to her, hell yes I will make love to you should have been my answer but that apprehension was still there. I pushed it away though because right now this amazing beautiful gorgeous woman wanted to have sex with me. My logical brain said I should wait and talk this out but what man thinks with his logical brain when sex is mentioned?

Siobhan led me into her bedroom then stopped beside her bed and turned to me, her eyes so full of trust. She stepped towards me, placing her hands on my chest and tipping her head back to look up at me. She was easily a foot shorter than me and the top of her head barely reached my shoulder.

I lifted my hands and smoothed her hair back from her face and pushed it over her shoulders. I couldn't wait to feel it on my chest and floating around us. I bent at the waist and buried my nose in the crook of her neck and shoulder, letting her hair cascade around my face like a golden curtain of silk.

She took a deep breath and tilted her head to the side and I lightly nipped her jaw and kissed my way back to her lips, sipping at them before I took her mouth in a deep kiss. I didn't take my time and ease into it, I buried my hand in her hair at the back of her head and tilted her the way I wanted her then took control.

Tipping my head one way and then another I tasted every inch of her mouth before I pulled back, both of us panting and out of breath.

Siobhan's hands were fisted in my shirt and I quickly reached behind me and pulled the shirt over my head, not bothering to undo the buttons up the front. She gasped a breath and fixed her gaze on my chest, then licked her lips and leaned forward, flattening her tongue on my nipple and licked it. I moaned as she bit me lightly then kissed across my chest to the other nipple. Fuck, I never though I liked that, but I sure as hell did now.

Before she could do any more I tipped her head up again and kissed her like I would die if I didn't. Her mouth was so sweet mixed with the spices from the meal she had made me and I couldn't get enough of her. My hands at her waist slowly slid upwards, pushing her t-shirt up with them until I got to her underarms, "Lift," I said, pushing her arms in the air so I could whip her shirt over her head.

She stood before me in nothing more than a pair of jeans, apparently having not put a bra on after her shower after work. Fuck if I'd known that we never would have sat at her kitchen table eating. Well, I would've been eating, but not the fish soup and meat pies. I knelt in front of her, my hands at her waist and kissed her belly, sliding my hands up to cup her breasts. They weren't big but they weren't small either and her nipples were hard and rosy. She moaned as I squeezed her tits in my hands and lightly pinched her nipples. She tipped her head down and let her hair cascaded down around us.

I undid the button and zipper on her jeans then stood and lifted her with me. I took a step towards the bed then dropped her on it and grabbed the waistband of her jeans and pulled them and her panties down her shapely legs. Her legs were full of muscle and were long and lean. The hair at the apex of her thighs was trimmed short and tidy and glistening with her arousal.

Before she could stop me I pushed her legs wide and buried my mouth in her pussy, licking her from the edge of her opening to her clit and sucked it into my mouth. Siobhan cried out and arched her hips off the bed.

I knew she had only been with one person before me so I knew she probably would be super tight and not used to stretching around a cock. And mine wasn't exactly small. I slid a finger into her tight sheath and stretched her, sliding another finger inside as I sucked on her clit, dragging an orgasm from her that had her muscles quivering and her breath whimpering from her in heavy pants.

Quickly before she could completely settle from her orgasm I shoved my pants off, pulling a condom from my wallet and fitting in on over my aching cock, then climbed over her and notched myself to her opening and paused. When she looked up at me, her pupils dilated and the green in her eyes almost swallowed by desire I asked, "Ready?" She nodded and I surged into her until I was buried to the hilt, balls deep in the most intense pleasure I'd ever felt.

Siobhan

"Oh my God!" I cried as I arched my back off the bed. I had thought Jaxon was going to thrust slowly and gently but as he filled me I couldn't help but be joyful at the feeling of him inside me. "Ooohhhh . . . that feels so good . . ."

"You sound surprised," He said, pulling back slightly to lean on his elbows on either side of my head so he could look in my eyes.

"I am surprised. The last time I did this I didn't enjoy it." I arched again and whimpered, "Please Jaxon, please move."

Jaxon took a deep shuddering breath and pulled out of me slowly then surged back in fast and hard. He kept that same pace, his gaze never leaving mine until I couldn't take it any longer and I closed my eyes, tipping my head back into the bed.

He leaned down and kissed my throat, sucking on my pulse point, nipping it then soothing the little bite with his tongue.

My hands couldn't stay still, I started gripping his biceps then slid my hands around his shoulders to feel the muscles in his back straining and flexing as he thrust into me over and over. One of his legs bent at the knee, pushing my leg higher and wider making his thrusts that much deeper and rubbing my clit between us with every push.

Jaxon wrapped his hands around my shoulders as his thrusts became faster and harder so I wouldn't slide up into the headboard and I reached down and gripped his cocked leg, digging my short nails into the back of his thigh.

He started to piston his hips faster and faster, grunting each time our hips met, then without pulling out of me he shifted back, pulling me with him until he was sitting back on his knees and my ass was up on his lap.

This position gave him all the power and I was arched off the bed so only my shoulders were touching the mattress. With each of his thrusts his cock touched deeper inside me, hitting my g-spot each time. I felt my inner muscles clench and tighten as my orgasm came hard and fast.

"Come on baby, cum with me . . . fuck baby, I can feel you cumming, let it go," He grunted, slamming into me again and again and then I was, I was coming and my back was bowed off the bed even more as the pleasure he was giving me ripped through my body.

Then without warning he slammed into me once more and arched his own back, throwing his head back and clenching his teeth, his jaw tight. I felt his cock twitch within me as he filled the condom with his cum and then he finally relaxed and leaned over me to kiss me gently on the lips.

Jaxon got up and quickly dealt with the condom then came back and crawled into bed beside me. He rolled over onto his back and pulled me across his chest. I was too spent to do anything other than lie there with him and listen to his deep breaths and his heart beating under my ear.

As I lazily traced the tattoos on his chest my fingertips came across a ridge of raised skin that tracked from one side of his chest to the other.

"What was this from?" I asked, tracing the scar. I felt him tense slightly then relax again as his heart slowed.

"I never told you why I started using did I?" He asked quietly and I shook my head no. "It's not a pretty story but if you want to hear it I'll tell you."

I lifted up off his chest to look into his eyes and smiled, "Jaxon, I want to hear your story. I want to know everything about you, but I can tell this is not an easy thing for you to tell. I don't need to hear all your dark secrets if it's easier for you to keep them hidden. I am happy with what we have right now and I can wait until you're ready to tell me if that's what you need."

He watched for intently for what felt like a full minute before he shook his head and smiled grimly.

"No, it's good for me to talk about it and you do need to know. It's ok, just come back here and cuddle up with me again." He said quietly. I did as he asked and snuggled into his chest, tracing his tattoos again.

"I only did two tours before I was done. The last time I was in Afghanistan we were only there to keep peace, we weren't really fighting. But one day Kabul got hit by a suicide bomber and we were in the city trying to help clean up the rubble and find survivors. I thought I had found a little girl buried under some concrete so I cleared as much of it away as I could. I found her hand and tried to pull her out but when I did the only part of her that came out was the arm I was pulling on."

He stopped talking when I gasped and my hand stilled. Then the hand he had resting on my back started to move, drawing lazy circles around my spine. He said nothing for a little while and I thought maybe that was the end of his story but I was wrong.

"Later the next day, we had finished with the cleanup and I hadn't slept much the night before because of the nightmares and my commanding officer called me out to the edge of our base. He just stood there staring out at the desert. He said something to me and I could tell he was hurting but I was too lost in my own grief and misery to figure it out and then he was pulling his weapon and he shot himself in the head. I was standing so close to him that when the bullet exited his head it streaked across my chest, leaving the scar."

I didn't say anything, I didn't move. I didn't think Jaxon needed me to talk right now. He shifted slightly, folding a pillow under his head and putting the hand that had been there over mine still resting on his chest.

"So, now you know." He whispered and I was sure he was trying to keep tears from slipping from the corners of his eyes. Slowly I levered up to look into his face and found the wetness trailing down over his temples. I reached up and wiped the tears away then leaned down and kissed his lips, trying to convey to him without words just how much his story touched my soul.

"Now I know," I whispered back. "And you're still the most amazing man I know. You obviously don't think so but you are so strong. I don't understand how more of you guys don't come back completely broken after serving in a war. I don't understand how more of you aren't addicts and suffering from PTSD. Cops suffer from PTSD, too but you guys, what you see, what you have to do and live through. Our government trains you to go over there and do what needs to be done but they don't train you how to deal with it afterwards. What you guys are doing at the MC is absolutely amazing, and I will forever be in awe of you and of your strength."

Jaxon didn't say anything, he just gazed at me, his eyes full of love and gratitude. He reached up and kissed me gently then pulled my head back to lie on his chest and hugged me tightly to him. We stayed that way until morning and I don't think either of us had slept so well before.

CHAPTER 9

Siobhan

The next morning I was up first but my moving around must have woken Jaxon up. I had gone to the bathroom and put on my robe that I almost never wore then went to the kitchen and made coffee.

When it was ready I carried two cups back to the bedroom and found Jaxon sitting on the bed in his underwear. I handed him a cup which he took with a smile and I sat beside him.

"Are you all right?" He asked as he took a sip, his eyes never leaving mine.

"Yes," I replied, confused that he would ask that. "I'm great, why?"

"Did you forget to tell me something last night? Did I hurt you?" He persisted, making me even more confused.

"No, you didn't hurt me at all, last night was amazing. Why would you ask that?"

"There's blood on the sheets." He said watching my face for my reaction.

"Oh," I said, drawing the word out. "Huh, you remember I said it had been a long time for me? And that the first person I was with I didn't enjoy sex with him?" Jaxon nodded and his eyebrows drew together as he frowned at me. "Well, that person and I only had sex once and it hurt so bad I made him stop before he finished and maybe he didn't get all the way in."

"So you're saying that technically you were still a virgin last night?"

"Uh, yeah I guess so, but honestly I didn't know for sure and I would have told you if I had." I rushed to assure him. I didn't lie, I don't lie and I wouldn't have lied about that. "I'm sorry; I really did think that whole virginity thing wasn't an issue anymore."

I shrugged and waited for him to respond. He watched me for a few seconds then leaned forward and kissed me gently.

"Who hurt you?" He asked seriously but I just shook my head. I wouldn't tell him, it didn't matter, that person was gone and really I didn't want to remember Dean in any way shape or form.

"It's done, it doesn't matter anymore and you've made it all better." I said smiling as he sipped his coffee. "Is that why you looked worried when I came in here? You thought you'd hurt me?"

"Yeah, that and I was, am worried about what happens with us when Lachlan is done with the MC." He said dipping his head to stare at the cup in his hands.

"I don't see how one has anything to do with the other." I said shrugging and he looked up at me sharply. "Seriously, what you and I are doing has nothing to do with Lachy getting clean . . . or not."

"So if Lachlan doesn't get clean, if what we're doing at the MC doesn't help him and he ends up back on the streets you're not going to hold that against me?"

Shit, how did I explain this?

Needles

Siobhan suddenly looked worried and my apprehension amped up with hers. She sighed and stood, putting her cup on the side table and started to pace.

"Here's the deal," she said, suddenly more serious than I had ever seen her, even when she was begging for her brother to have a chance at our program. "I know and completely understand that Lachy's sobriety isn't conditional on anything you do or don't do. I know that the only variable that matters in this is Lachy and the choices he makes from here on out. I know that, I do, I know that now and I'll know that then if he relapses.

"Even knowing that I will still be upset if Lachy does relapse and part of the reason for that is because I made up my mind that if he didn't do what needed to be done to get and stay clean this time I had to cut him out of my life. Will I be upset?" she continued still pacing, "Yes, incredibly, he's my baby brother. But I will know that his choices and decisions are not on you and that you are no more responsible for his choices then me.

"If Lachy relapses then I will probably yell and scream and cry and swear and I might even shut down or shut you out for a while but it won't be because I blame you or the MC. It'll be because to me my baby brother will have just died and I'll have to learn how to deal with that and live with that."

I put my coffee cup beside hers on the table and stood, walking to where she stopped pacing across the room. I stopped in front of her and cupped her face in my hands. I gently rubbed my thumbs over his cheek bones and her eyes drifted closed until I leaned forward and rested my forehead on hers.

"Please know that the members of the MC who are involved with the center the most are doing everything they can to help Lachlan make the best decisions for his health and sobriety." I said seriously. "You also need to know that if you ever need anything, if it's just to yell or fight or scream or cry I am here for you to vent on. If you need space I can give you that too, as long as you shutting me out isn't a forever thing. Please let me help you through this if it turns bad and please don't lose hope that Lachlan will make the right choices. Your hope might be all he has left."

She nodded as a single tear drifted down her cheek and I bent to kiss it away. I kissed lightly over her face until I finally reached her lips and kissed her briefly but deeply before I pulled back to look at her.

"I have to go to work today, do you want to stop by the shop and we'll go for lunch later?" she smiled and nodded, winding her arms around my neck, forcing my hands from her face to move down her back so I reached farther and cupped her ass.

"I'd love to go to lunch with you," She said, the wetness in her eyes gone but a happy gleam replacing it. "And see where you work." I dipped my head and kissed her again then turned and started to get dressed. I needed to run home and shower before I went to work so I needed to get going.

Hours later I was sitting in the shop with Lix talking to Ashlyn, Pixie's little sister. Siobhan had texted a few minutes ago saying she was on her way for lunch so I wasn't starting anything new but I was watching Lix work on Ash. She wasn't getting anything major, just a small stylized pixie reaching for the stars on the back of her shoulder.

I knew it was for her sister Grace-Lynn whose nickname was Pixie. I also knew that Grace-Lynn was getting a tattoo in the same style of a phoenix rising from the ashes. She said it was to symbolize the time they had lost but had stayed sisters to the end.

"Ash, Lix here said you might want to become an artist?" I said suddenly watching her face. Lix wasn't paying any attention to us and since he couldn't hear us I thought this was the perfect time to mention it.

"Um, I've thought about it," She said, shrugging slightly as Lix took the needle away from her shoulder to wipe the area clean. "I love to draw, I just don't know how good I'd be at the tattooing part."

"It definitely takes practice." I said thoughtfully as the chime above the door went off. "Think about it, I'd like to see some of your art, maybe you can start off just designing and working the front. But you're under eighteen so I need to know that your dad is ok with you working here." She nodded and I stood to walk out front to greet whoever had just come in.

I had hoped it would be Siobhan but I wasn't so lucky. It was the slimy lawyer she had kneed the day we took Lachlan from the jail to the hospital. We knew each other in passing but had never taken the time to get to know each other. Sharpie, the club lawyer had never had anything good to say about the guy.

"Can I help you?" I asked, trying really hard to be polite, if a bit standoffish. The guy was probably only an inch shorter than I was but I was pretty sure he was wearing lifts in his shoes. His suit was impeccable with the creases in his pants and the perfectly matching tie. He placed his hands wide with his fingers spread on the counter and leaned towards me.

"Yeah, you can stay the fuck away from Siobhan MacDonald." He said but didn't stay in my space. As quickly as he leaned in he leaned out then shot the cuffs of his dress shirt and smirked. "She's mine."

I don't usually look for fights, I've had my fair share and won more than my share but I rarely threw the first punch. With this guy, though I would have been happy to knock a few of his perfect teeth out. I took a step back from the counter and shoved my hands into my pockets so I wouldn't be tempted to actually punch him.

That's when I realized the pin I kept in my pocket was gone. Shit!

"That's what I thought," The guy said when I didn't answer right away. "She's not that good a lay anyway, but she's still mine."

I saw red then and would have jumped over the counter and killed him if the bells above the door hadn't rang at that exact moment.

CHAPTER 10

Siobhan

I stood on the sidewalk looking up at the sign for Jaxon's shop. WAMC Tattoos, that's it, nothing flashy or extravagant. I knew he owned the shop and not the MC but he had still chosen to name his store after the MC who had saved him. I smiled at his sentimentality and took a deep breath, pulling the front door open and stepping inside.

Unfortunately what I found when I stepped inside made my insides shrivel.

"She's not that good a lay anyway, but she's still mine." Dean said and I could hear the smirk in his voice. I could also see Jaxon about to fly over the counter and kill Dean.

"It's hard to be any good at something when the person you're doing it with doesn't listen to you when you say he's hurting you." I said caustically as I rounded the counter to stand beside Jaxon. "Or when the person who's hurting you is telling you to shut up and stop crying." Jaxon had pulled his hands out of his pockets and was flexing them into fists.

"What are you doing here Dean?" I demanded, putting my hand on Jaxon's back hoping to calm him a little.

"Just came to see where you were slumming." He said, smirking again.

"You hurt her?" Jaxon growled at Dean.

"Oh please," Dean scoffed back, "It always hurts the first time."

"Not if you do it properly." Jaxon snarled, my calming hand on his back was not doing the trick so I stepped in front of him and put a hand on his chest, pushing him back.

"Stop," I said with a gentle shove.

"Get the fuck out of my shop and don't come back. Stay the fuck away from Siobhan."

"Gladly, but I will have her again, you just wait." Dean laughed, pointing at me before he walked out of the store.

"He hurt you." Jaxon snarled down at me accusingly. I nodded then lifted up on my toes and kissed him lightly on the lips.

"But you fixed it, you made it all better." I whispered, feeling more than seeing him calm down. "You left something at my house today."

I stepped back slightly and pulled the strange thing I'd found out of my back pocket. It was like a key ring with a bobby pin hanging on it but I could tell that wasn't what it was. I was trained in different kinds of weaponry and that included grenades. I knew a grenade pin when I saw it.

"You um, carry that around for a reason?"

Jaxon stood for the longest time looking down at the pin in my hand. His hands were still balled into tight fists but slowly his right hand loosened and he reached to take the pin from me. He looked at it a bit longer in his own hand before he slipped it into his pocket.

"I found that the day of that bomb in Kabul. With everything that happened that day and the day after I just kept it. I kept it while I was on the street and using and at my worst. I held that while I was in detox and going through withdrawal and I hold that when the PAWS is the worst. It doesn't do anything to physically help but for some reason just having it helps."

I nodded, understanding what he was saying and knowing that it didn't have to make sense for it to help him. PAWS was much like PTSD in soldiers and trauma victims but was associated with recovering addicts.

It stood for post-acute withdrawal syndrome. He was completely calmed down now, to the point of exhaustion and I knew he needed sleep more than he needed food. I reached up and cupped his cheek and he raised his tired and weary gaze to mine.

"Come on, I'll take you home so you can get some sleep." I said smiling up at him.

"I can't leave, Lix has got a full schedule." He said, shaking his head.

A throat cleared behind us and we both turned to see a young girl standing in the doorway to the back rooms.

"I can stay and help Lix," she said smiling shyly. "Um, maybe a sort of trial run to see if I want to work here? Or to see if I can do it and you really want me to work here?"

Jaxon nodded and started towards the back room. "I'll just tell Lix the plan then and call in another guy to help out."

Needles

We drove in silence all the way to the clubhouse. I had told Siobhan it wasn't necessary for her to drive me but she insisted and really I was thankful. I could feel a migraine coming on and I didn't know if I would make it to the clubhouse on my own before it hit full force. I sat with my eyes closed and my head tipped back and resting on the headrest of the passenger seat.

"We're here," She said quietly as she put the car into park. "Do you want me to come inside or just go?"

My eyes jerked open and I whipped my head around to look at her then winced when the movement jarred my head.

"I don't ever want you to go," I rasped, squinting at the bright sunlight. "But this isn't going to be a fun night. I can feel a migraine coming on and I can't take anything for it."

"Come on," She said turning the car off and getting out. I followed her lead and met her at the front of the car. "Let's go, I'll help you get comfortable in your room." I smiled slightly at her then led her into the building, heading towards the hall that led to the private rooms.

"What's this?" a voice boomed from across the main room of the clubhouse. "Little Needles has a woman! Is Little Needles going to share his woman?"

Laughter followed the voice and a couple of the other guys sitting around the table chuckled. I looked over at the table and saw Buster. He wasn't a full member of the club but he came and hung out with his cronies every-so-often.

"Fuck off," I muttered to Buster and kept walking, pulling Siobhan with me.

"Awe! Come on! Me and the boys want a piece of that sweet little ass!" Buster called and cackled. I was about to turn and go beat the shit out of him when Siobhan stopped me. Then she turned and walked over to the table. "Heh, little Needles, your woman would rather have a real man, eh?"

"Stand up." Siobhan demanded when she stood in front of the much bigger man. Buster stood at least as tall as I did and outweighed me by close to fifty pounds. I stood leaning against the bar, knowing Siobhan could take care of herself.

I glanced over as Lo and Axle came out of the office to see what was going on. They both sent me a nod to let me know they were there to help if it was needed.

"I said stand up." Siobhan repeated when Buster just guffawed at her.

Finally he rose slowly to his feet and glared down at her. Before he could move or speak she had planted her knee between his legs. When he was bent over clutching his aching balls she slammed her fist into his cheek bone and he slumped to the floor. He rolled over to his back still clutching his crotch and she stepped on his neck.

"Just for your information, Little Needles is a giant compared to you, and no his woman doesn't want you because you are not a real man. Also, I'm a cop so shut up before I arrest you for uttering threats against a police officer."

Siobhan stepped off of Buster and walked over to me as Lo and Axle clapped. She tipped her head to them then took my hand. As we left the main room I heard Lo tell Buster to get out of the club-house, take his friends with him and never come back, he was no longer welcome.

I led Siobhan to my room and let us in then slumped on my bed moaning at the pain in my head. As I lay there dying she rushed around the room closing the blinds on my window and turning off anything that emitted light of any kind. Then she pulled my boots off my feet and undid my shirt and my pants but left them both on.

She made me roll over to the middle of the bed so I sat up and pulled my shirt and pants off myself then lay back down again. Siobhan pulled the blanket she had pulled out from under me when I sat up, over me to my chin then sat beside me on the bed.

"Does anything help when you get like this?" she asked quietly, smoothing her hand over my forehead. I couldn't see her in the darkness except for her outline.

"No," I whispered and tried to breathe through the pain. "You

PINS AND NEEDLES

don't have to stay, I'm probably going to get sick at some point and it's not pretty. Just leave the light on in the bathroom."

"Don't be silly, I'm not leaving you." She said like it was the stupidest thing she'd ever heard. "You wouldn't leave me."

Before I knew what she was doing she had the bottom of my blanket pulled off my feet and my socks off. Then she was rubbing certain spots on my feet. At first the pain in my head swelled but then subsided enough that I could bear it. Siobhan switched from one point to another, from foot to foot and eventually I fell asleep.

Slowly I woke to the combined scents of flowers and mint. My forehead was warm and wet but the pain in my head was almost gone. I took a deep breath and cracked my eyes open. Siobhan was lying beside me with her back against my side but she stirred when I turned my head towards her.

"You're awake," She said smiling sleepily.

"Why do I smell like flowers and toothpaste?" I whispered.

"Lavender and mint oil, both help with migraine pain." She replied chuckling.

"You just carry those around with you?"

"My mom gets migraines and doesn't like the way the medications prescribed for them make her feel so we found other ways to help with the pain." She said, shrugging. "I always have some of each in my car and my dad and I learned the pressure points to give her some relief."

"Mmm," I murmured, rubbing a hand over my face, smearing the oils all over. "Do I remember you kicking Buster's ass earlier today?"

"Yesterday? Yes if that large odious man was Buster."

"That was yesterday? How long did I sleep?" Siobhan shifted and checked the clock on her phone.

"It is currently eight in the morning so you slept a good sixteen hours."

"Holy shit," I muttered, sitting up slowly. "Did I get sick?"

"I don't think so," Siobhan answered sitting up beside me. "At least not while I was in here and if you did when I was out in the kitchen you cleaned it up, but from the time I left to the time I came back in it didn't look like you had moved."

"Shit, I'm sorry. You didn't have to stay." I said though I was grateful she had. "You must have been bored. Did you find something to do at least? And eat?"

"Oh yeah," She said shrugging. "I got a little curious so I checked things out. I don't think I went into anyone's private space but I did find the kitchen, and met Alana, Brooke, Kat and Pixie there. They're super cool."

"Yeah, they really are." I said nodding and smiling. "Did they have the kids with them?"

"No, but I heard all about them. Alana's five boys and one girl, Brooke's little girl and Kat's three. Wow, that's a lot of kids. Pixie said something about doing a test in the morning so I think that means she thinks she's pregnant."

"Yeah, her and Seether have been trying to have a baby and haven't had any luck getting pregnant." I rubbed my hand over my face again before I remembered I was covered in the fragrant oils. "I think I need a shower."

"You go ahead, I'm gonna head home."

"Do you have to?" I asked, hopefully. "I have an extra toothbrush if you want, I can make you breakfast here and then if you don't mind you could drive me to the shop to pick up my bike. Then we could spend the day together if you're not too sick of me."

"I'm not sick of you at all," She said, shaking her head and smiling. "That actually sounds like a pretty good plan. I will take you up on that toothbrush though."

CHAPTER 11

Siobhan

Just over a week since Jaxon's migraine and I was back at the club-house only this time it was for a party. An adults only party. I decided this was a good time to introduce Casey to the MC. She had been begging me to bring her along so I figured what could possibly go wrong. Damn, what a foolish thought.

When I got to her house to pick her up, she came rushing outside in stiletto heels and a tight leather mini skirt. I got out of my car and stood in the door and told her to turn around and go back and change.

"What?" she demanded angrily, "It took me all day to figure out this outfit!"

"Go put some pants and normal shoes on." I said, crossing my arms over my chest. "Or I'm not taking you." She huffed and actually stomped her foot then turned and walked back into her house and slammed the door, then opened it again and stuck her head out.

"Get in here and help me!" she hollered at me then disappeared again. I laughed at her and hurried in to help her get dressed in clothing more befitting a woman of her age and high amount of self-respect.

She ended up with the same backless sequined top and black leggings with tall boots. She looked hot regardless of what she was wearing. I was almost jealous, but I knew I looked good in my skinny jeans and tight sweater, and I knew Jaxon would only have eyes for me anyway.

Casey and I got into my car and drove out to the clubhouse, singing like crazy people to the radio the entire way.

"So what's this party for?" Casey finally asked as we pulled into the parking lot of the club house.

"Jaxon didn't tell me." I shrugged. "Does it matter?"

"Hells no!" Casey cried as she got out of the car.

When we made it into the clubhouse I immediately looked for Jaxon and found him at the bar with a glass of dark liquid, probably Coke and before I could make it over to him Casey was whisked away from me by one of the members who dragged her onto the dance floor. Jaxon made his way over to me as I watched Casey and her new friend dance and slid a hand around my waist.

"That's Nick, he's harmless." Jaxon said in my ear and kissed my temple. I turned to ask him how Nick had such a normal name when his mouth covered mine and he kissed me deeply. He growled low in his throat before he pulled back and nipped my bottom lip then soothed it with his tongue. "I missed you."

"Mm, I missed you, too." I breathed, stretching up on my toes to kiss him again, tangling my tongue with his until someone bumped him from behind and knocked us off balance a bit. Before either of us could say anything else Casey bounded up to us and wrapped us in a group hug.

"It's yummy!" She cried smiling widely.

"Jaxon, this is Casey," I said, snorting at her calling him yummy to his face. "Casey, this is Needles."

"Ooo, big bad biker name!" Casey smirked as she stared up at Jaxon. He smiled down at her, as tall as Casey was he was still taller by a couple of inches.

"Casey!" We all turned to see who had bellowed Casey's name

from across the room and found Nick standing on a chair waving her over.

"Gotta go!" She exclaimed and dashed off to join Nick.

"Is he really harmless?"

"Yeah, he's really harmless. His road name is Saint because his name is Nicholas and he's constantly giving money to kids and helping out with children's charities and stuff. Saint Nicholas is the patron saint of children. You should have seen him overseas, I'm told he was a favorite among the local children."

"Huh, that's nice." I said absently watching Casey and Nick. "So, what is this party for?"

"Well, we usually have bar-b-ques when we have something to celebrate but it's gotten too cold out." I nodded, agreeing that the end of October was not the best time to have a bar-b-que.

"But what are we celebrating?"

"Pixie's pregnant, three months, she said."

"What? But she just said last week that she was doing a test!"

"I don't know," Jaxon said holding his hands up in surrender, "I'm just repeating what I was told."

"I gotta find her, where is she?"

"I think her and Seether are over by the pool tables," Jaxon said nodding in that direction. "At least that's where Seether is and it looks like Pixie's red hair next to him. You go over, I'll bring you a Diet Coke."

Needles

Siobhan left me and hurried over to where I pointed out Seether as I went over for a refill on my Coke and to grab her a Diet, no ice. As I was standing at the bar a hand snaked up my back and grabbed the back of my neck.

"You hurt her and I will kill you." I turned to see Casey standing close to me, a wicked gleam in her eye. "I mean it, she's the best friend I've ever had and that douche Dean really did a number on her. I have six older brothers, one is a doctor and one is a pharmacist, I know how to kill you and make it look like an accident, if you're even ever found."

With that she turned and was gone, presumably looking for Nick. Holy shit, that was kind of scary.

"What was that about?" Siobhan asked, walking over to join me at the bar.

"Uh, your girl just threatened my life." I replied, still watching Casey dance away.

"Ah, Casey, such a great friend," Siobhan said smiling. "Dean just laughed at her when she told him that, I'm glad to see you're suitably afraid. Did she mention her brothers?"

"Yeah, the doctor and the pharmacist?"

"Oh, she forgot about the hockey player, the logger and the Spec. Ops soldier."

"Ok," I said perplexed, "I get why the soldier is scary, but why the hockey player and the logger? And that's only five, what about the sixth brother?"

"The hockey player is an enforcer, he'll kill you with his stick and the logger has chainsaws, nough said? The youngest brother is backpacking across Europe or something like that." Siobhan shrugged. I snorted and nodded then laughed with her.

"Don't worry," I said, pulling her close to whisper in her ear, "I won't ever hurt you, I think I'm gonna want to keep you around for a very long time." I nipped her earlobe then sucked it into my mouth, swirling my tongue around her earring. She moaned and clenched her thighs together, making me chuckle darkly. "What did Pixie say?"

"Who?" Siobhan asked absently, "Oh, right, she said her cycle has never been regular so she didn't realize that she was pregnant when she missed her periods, she just thought she was off again."

"Cool, TMI but cool." I said nodding. "Now that you've seen the guest of honor you think we could duck out?"

"Mm, what about Casey?"

"I think she's fine with Nick but if you want to go over and say goodbye and tell her Nick will find her an empty bedroom to crash in if she wants it." I replied, cupping Siobhan's ass and pulling her into my quickly hardening cock.

"K," Siobhan breathed then kissed me like she wanted to rip my clothes off right here and now. When she pulled away I growled but she hurried over to Casey to tell her the plan.

Nick said something to her, pulling Casey into him who turned and bit his neck, making him squirm and laugh. Siobhan shook her head at the two of them then hurried back over to me and took my hand, pulling me behind her to my room.

When we got there she turned and put her back against the door, pulling me against her front and pulling my head down to kiss her. She was so short I had to bed almost double to do it so I lifted her and wrapped her legs around my waist, trapping her against the door. I pushed my cock into the juncture of her thighs, rubbing against her like I wanted to do naked.

"Mm, Jaxon, hurry . . ." she panted arching against me. "We have too many clothes on . . . please baby, open the door." I kissed her again and reached into my back pocket for my keys to unlock the door. When it swung open I carried her inside and slammed it closed with my foot then leaned back against it, still holding her.

"Get naked, fast." I ordered as I placed her gently on her feet then started undoing the buttons on my shirt.

Siobhan lifted the hem of her sweater and pulled it over her head, dropping it to the floor beside her. She lifted one of her feet and placed it on the edge of the bed, unzipping her boot then pulled it off and did the same with the other one then slowly, as though she was trying to torture me, undid her pants and slid them down her hips and her legs.

When she had her pants around her knees she turned her back and bent, pushing her pants all the way down to her ankles.

"Fuck . . ." I breathed then reached forward to cup her ass in my hands and massaged the full globes. "I'm gonna fuck you like this, you ok with that?"

"Oh yeah," She gasped, throwing her head back, her hair flying into the air as she rocked back into me. "You're still wearing too many clothes." I gently pushed her so she fell onto the bed and yanked her pants off her feet then undid the button and fly of my own jeans, shoving them down my legs.

I stood in front of her as she looked her fill, then sat up and took my cock in her hand. Just as I was about to tell her not to, she flicked her tongue out and licked the tip of my cock, taking a drop of pre-cum with her.

I pulled her hand away and pushed her to lie back on the bed. Her legs were dangling over the edge and she was in the perfect position.

"Put your feet on the edge of the bed." I rasped, lifting one of her legs to help her.

With her feet like this she was spread so wide for me. I could see her pretty pussy around the edges of her thong panties. Her sweet flesh was wet and glistening with her desire.

I knelt in front of her and licked her over her panties then fit my finger under the edge of them and pulled them out of the way so I could lick her and taste her. Soon she was writhing under my mouth, completely unable to keep quiet so I bit her clit gently and pushed two fingers inside her, rubbing that spot just inside her tight sheath.

Siobhan exploded around my fingers and flooded my mouth with her taste. I quickly stood and pulled a condom out of my night stand and slid it on then laid over her and surged into her hard and fast. She cried out again as she came around me harder than before.

"Fuck … you're so fucking amazing," I gasped, pumping in and out of her quickly, twisting my hips as I thrust inside, and rubbing her clit, still sensitive from my mouth. "Wait, I have an idea … "

Siobhan

I didn't know what Jaxon had planned but when he pulled away and said he had an idea then pulled my panties off I thought I was ready for anything. He pulled me off the bed and lifted me into his arms, kissing me as he walked us into the bathroom. I whimpered against his mouth, my pussy clenching, missing his thickness inside me.

Jaxon put my feet on the floor and pulled away to start the shower then adjusted the temperature so it was warm enough then pulled me into the tub behind him, closing the curtain. I decided then I liked this idea of his but I didn't know it all yet.

He pushed me back against the cold tile and before I could squeak he turned me and pushed my breasts against the wall. The cold tile after the warm water was a shock that had me gasping as my nipples hardened.

I tried to pull my hands up to push against the tile to get closer to him but he held them behind my back. I was essentially his prisoner to do with what he wanted. Knowing he would never hurt me and I only needed to say stop and he would turn me on so much I thought I was going to cum from that alone.

Jaxon's free hand was not still. It roamed my body and pinched and squeezed and teased until I thought I might explode. Eventually his fingers slid between the cheeks of my ass and played with my hole until I was pushing against his finger, needing more, then his hand slid down the back of my thigh, lifting my leg so my foot rested on the edge of the tub.

Before I could ask what he meant to do he was thrusting up inside of me, my nipples abrading the tile as he lifted me higher with each trust, only my toes touching the bottom of the tub.

I pulled gently on my hands and he let them go, wrapping his hand around my waist and holding my stomach and he pumped his hips into me. I couldn't take the sensations of heat at my back and cold at my front anymore so I leaned back against him, completely boneless, letting him take what he wanted.

Jaxon's hand at my waist slipped down my front to press on my clit and I had to lift my arms to wind them around his neck to keep myself upright as waves of pleasure floated over me.

When my inner muscles started to clench Jaxon grunted and his hands flexed around me. He thrust twice more and stopped, buried so deep inside me I could feel him twitching against my cervix.

"Holy fuck, baby," Jaxon whispered in my ear as he slipped out of me and his hands snaked all over my body. "You're fucking amazing."

"I didn't really do anything, Jaxon," I chuckled tiredly, letting him take my weight as I slumped against him. "That was a great idea though."

CHAPTER 12

Siobhan

My next shift was two days after the party at the clubhouse. I had met Casey in the kitchen in the morning and she swears she spent the night with Nick but they didn't have sex. I choose to believe her, she's crazy not stupid. So, here I was clocking in for my first night shift of five. Jaxon had worked his schedule at the shop so that he was off on the same days I was so we could spend as much time together as possible.

He always started our days with updates on my brother. Apparently Lachy was doing well, detox and withdrawals were over and he was stepping up and making an effort with all the activities the center had him doing. And he was even talking to the counsellors.

There were two, one was Brooke but she hadn't finished her clinical degree so she was always assisting the clinical counsellor. The guys and even one girl at the center were accepting Lachy more now that they knew some of his story.

I knew from what Jaxon had said Lachy hadn't told them everything. I believe that I am the only person besides Lachy and the person who hurt him who knows the whole story.

So, now here I am standing at my desk looking at the mess. I looked up and around the office but everyone was busy with something and no one looked back at me. This wasn't my desk. I wasn't generally a neat freak but my work space was always tidy. This wasn't tidy.

There were food wrappers and empty drink containers everywhere, papers were piled haphazardly and as I stood there staring one of them actually fell onto the floor. That at least got some attention as a few people closest to me looked up in shock.

"Who the hell was using my desk?" I demanded looking around.

"Ask the commander," was the reply I got from those around me. I heaved a sigh and went to the night shift commander's office hoping for answers. I knocked and was told to enter.

"Sir, may I ask –"

"You've been transferred." The commander said without letting me actually ask.

"I'm sorry sir? I didn't put in for a transfer." I replied confused.

"Doesn't matter, your particular skills are needed somewhere else." The Commander stated without even looking up at me. "Your things were cleaned out of your desk and your cases were given to another Constable." He pointed over to a small office box in the corner of his room. "Report to K9 immediately."

"Yes sir," I sighed knowing better than to argue with the Commanding officer. I grabbed my little box and hurried down to the K9 unit offices, stopping at the front desk. "Hi, I'm Constable Siobhan MacDonald, I was told to report here for duty."

"Oh," the receptionist said looking at me with shock. "We don't have any paperwork for you that I know of and our Commander is off tonight."

"You don't have a night shift Commander?"

"Not right now?"

"Are you asking me that?"

"No," the lady said. "Look, I don't know what's going on but I don't have the paperwork for you to transfer. The only thing I can tell you is to go back to your last duty station and ask them what is going on."

"Awesome," I sighed, I really didn't need this. "Thank you for your help."

The lady smiled pleasantly and I headed back up to my previous commander's office. He was busy with something and I had to wait an hour before I could see him. Finally when I was allowed into his office it was because him and Dean were walking out laughing with each other. Both men gave me a look that said I wasn't finished running around tonight.

"Come on in Constable MacDonald." The commander said when Dean had finally left. "Why are you back?"

"I'm sorry sir, I went down to K9 and they don't have any transfer information for me and their commander is not in the office right now. Has there possibly been a mistake?"

"Are you saying I lied?" the commander's eyebrows shot up his forehead.

"No sir I am not. I am only asking if somewhere in the channels my paperwork is delayed or lost."

"Huh," the commander grunted and started shuffling through the papers on his desk. "Well here's the problem MacDonald. You said K9? I sent you to the motor pool."

"I'm sorry?"

"Says right here MacDonald, motor pool. Here, take this," He handed me a sheaf of papers and waved me away. "Take that to the motor pool, if your orders have been lost somewhere you can show them that."

"Yes sir," I said and turned to leave, still carrying my box of things. I hurried down to the motor pool offices in the parking garage of the building and stopped at reception. "Hi, I'm Constable Mac-Donald, I was told to report here for duty."

"Yes Constable, you are late, we expected you over an hour ago." The receptionist said tsking her displeasure.

"Yes, I'm sorry, I was accidently sent to K9 then had to wait an hour for my actual assignment. I apologize." I said knowing better than to blame my previous Commander. "Also I was told to bring this to you in case of any confusion."

I handed over the papers the Commander had given me and stood waiting to be told where to go and what to do. I had never worked in the motor pool before so I didn't know what I should do.

"This is a file we've been waiting for, not sure how this would clear up any confusion involving you." The receptionist snarked. I frowned and shook my head.

"Again I apologize, that was what I was told." I was really getting tired of this run around and after seeing Dean with the Commander I knew he was at the bottom of it.

"Well, go to your desk. There's an empty one back there somewhere." The lady said waving a hand over her shoulder. She buzzed me back so I could open the waist high door to get behind the counter. I put my box on the first empty desk I came to, or so I thought.

"Not that one." The receptionist called over her shoulder. I tried three more before I finally got frustrated and turned to her.

"How about you just tell me which desk I can use?" She turned in her chair and the gleam in her eye was a little more respectful.

"The one beside that one will be just fine." She said then turned and ignored me some more. I emptied my box but when I lifted out the picture of Lachy and I the glass in the frame was broken.

"Sons of bitches!" I hissed angrily.

My temper was quickly rising to the top and I was having trouble breathing through my frustration. It really wasn't going to take much to make me explode right now.

"Pardon me?" The receptionist asked, turning around in her chair to give me an imperious look.

"What is your name?"

"Edna."

"Well Edna, when the assholes upstairs decided they were going to transfer me they packed up my desk and broke one of the only happy pictures of my brother and I that I have. I'm a little frustrated right now since I didn't ask for this transfer and I'm pretty sure it came at the request of my ex-boyfriend because I didn't sleep with him and I'm not seeing someone else. So please, Edna, how about you just tell me what the hell I'm supposed to be doing down here right now?"

"Nothing," Edna shrugged. "I'm the only one who works nights."

"Then why did you give me hell when I came in late?"

"Because I was expecting you much earlier than when you arrived, it's not like I just sit here doing nothing waiting for difficult cops to show up all night."

"Thank you Edna." I said, sighing heavily. "What time am I supposed to report in the morning?"

"Six a.m." she replied, turning back to her desk. I looked at my watch; it was now ten p.m. and after sleeping most of the day to get ready for this shift I probably wouldn't be able to sleep tonight to get ready for the next shift.

"Are these shifts ten hours?"

"No, five eights," She replied, not turning around.

"So tomorrow being Wednesday is my first of five shifts? And is there a rotation so everyone gets the weekend off at some point?"

"No," Edna snorted, spinning around in her chair again. "You're here to cover the weekend so the more senior officers can have it off."

"That's fantastic, thank you so much for your help Edna." I said as I slammed out of the office and back to my car.

Needles

It was six days before I heard from Siobhan again. This was strange as she usually texted me when she got up for her shift and before she went to bed. For the last six days I had barely an emoji text from her and it was never more than a wave. I was getting worried so I asked Nick for Casey's number and texted her.

U herd from S?

> **She was transferred to the motor pool**
> **It totally messed up her sched.**

She askd 4 a transfer?

> **Nope, she was informed of the change**

She ok?

> **As she can be considering her skeevy**
> **Ex-boyfriend requested the move for her.**

Fuck

> **Yes, got to go, got a call, ttyl**

I was kind of shocked to say the least. Why would Dean Zane have so much pull at the police detachment that he could get Siobhan transferred when she hadn't requested it and she had an exemplary record? Something wasn't right here but I knew I had to step back and let Siobhan deal with it. She wouldn't appreciate me stepping in to fix it for her, if I even could.

So, I went about my day and continued to send her texts letting her know I was there when she was ready to talk. Eventually she did send me a message asking me to stop by her house when I could. I was on my way there now having dropped everything I was working on. Luckily I didn't have a client in my chair at the time.

"Hey," I said when she opened her front door. She smiled slightly then turned and walked back into her house and slumped onto the couch. She had obviously spent quite a bit of time on her couch. Her usually tidy house was a mess with takeout containers on the coffee table and a blanket and pillow spread out on the couch. "You ok?"

"No," she replied from where she'd buried herself in her blankets. "I'm not ok. Dean had me transferred to the motor pool and their schedule is very different than I'm used to and it's taken me four of the five days that I was on shift to get on that schedule. I'm on my second day off now and I'm exhausted. I have to go back to work tomorrow and I'm seriously considering quitting."

"Siobhan," I said shocked. I crouched in front of her on the couch and pushed her blanket back a bit so I could see her face. "You love being a cop, why would you quit?"

"You're right," she huffed and sat up. "I do love being a cop, I do not love sitting around waiting for another cop to bring his patrol cruiser in so I can fill it up with gas or clean up the puke in the back, or the blood or the piss or the myriad of other nasty things that could be back there."

"What the hell is going on?" I asked sitting in the space beside her.

"I don't know; I haven't been able to figure it out. I only know that Dean has something to do with it." She sighed dejected. "My first shift after the party I went in and my desk was a mess. I went to my commander to ask what the hell and he said I'd been transferred to K9 and there was a box of my stuff in the corner.

"So fine, I went down to K9 and they said they knew nothing about me being transferred there. So I went back to my commander and had to wait over an hour while he talked and laughed with Dean who came out of his office and smirked at me then left. I asked my Commander for clarification and he said the problem was that he had told me motor pool, not K9. Then he hands me a file to take down there telling me it's my transfer papers. I get to motor pool and the receptionist there gives me hell for being late, takes the file that has nothing to do with me and tells me to find a desk.

"After trying three empty desks she finally tells me which one I can use then says motor pool doesn't have a night shift and my shift starts at six in the morning. I'm the extra that covers the weekends and since I'm the newest on the shift I get to clean up the worst of the messes. It's fucking awesome and I'm so fucking done."

When she was done talking Siobhan fell to the side and dropped her head on my shoulder. I could tell she was exhausted and frustrated but I was still surprised when I felt her hot wet tears drop onto my shirt.

"Oh baby," I said turning and pulling her into my arms. She cried silently for a few minutes then sniffed and pulled away, wiping at her eyes.

"I'm sorry, I guess talking about it all like that just finally got to me."

"You haven't been able to find out what's going on?" I asked, smoothing her hair down her back.

She shook her head and sniffed again. "I've had everyone I can think of who might be able to find out and would actually tell me, asking what is going on. No one has been able to give me any answers. They just shrug and say sorry."

"Besides the puke and other bodily fluids, is motor pool that bad?"

"It's not motor pool really, although I didn't do all the training I did so I could pump gas. And I'm not treated badly per se, but whenever a really bad car comes in it's automatically dropped on my desk to do. I go into work in the morning and my desk is a mess like someone ate there and left their garbage but I know Edna is the only one there at night and she would never do that." Siobhan shrugged and sighed again, slouching against the back of the couch.

"I'm sorry baby, is there anything I can do?"

"No, just this, just hang out with me and hold me. I just don't know what to do." She said cuddling into me.

"Do you really want to quit the force?"

"I don't know. If I wasn't stuck in motor pool we wouldn't even be having this conversation. If I had been transferred to K9 we wouldn't be having this conversation. I loved being a cop but right now I'm not being a cop. I'm sorry I ignored you for a week."

"I'm sorry hun, I don't know what to tell you." I said rubbing her shoulder and squeezing her tight. "You didn't ignore me, don't worry about it. I talked to Casey so I knew something was up and you needed some time. Do you want me to stay tonight?" I asked, filtering my fingers through the hair at her temple.

"To sleep?"

"Absolutely, I really just want to hold you." She sighed and melted into me, falling asleep almost immediately. It was only about six in the evening and I hadn't eaten supper yet. I moved Siobhan to her bed and tidied the living room a little while a freezer dinner she had stashed away was warming in the microwave.

I quickly ate it while I texted Lo, asking if he could find out what was going on at the detachment with Siobhan's transfer. By then it was eight and while I wasn't tired I missed Siobhan so much I crawled into bed with her just to hold her.

By morning I was jolted away at 4:30 by the alarm on Siobhan's phone and her moaning about having to get up. She sighed and rolled slowly out of bed and jumped in the shower, leaving her alarm ringing. I turned it off and went into the kitchen to start a pot of coffee. By the time it was ready she was rushing out of her room dressed in her uniform, pulling her hair back into the tight bun she always kept it in.

Siobhan sighed with happiness as I handed her a travel mug of hot black coffee and kissed me deeply.

"Here," she said, pulling out her key ring. "I had this made a couple of weeks ago; it's an extra key to the house. Go back to bed, stay as long as you want, come back when you want, I'm usually off by 2:30 if nothing disgusting happens in the back of a car that needs extra time."

And then she was gone, rushing out the door and to work. Huh, a key to her house. What did this mean? Did she want me to move in? No, that's not it; it was just easier for me to have a key in case anything was going on, right?

Shit, I needed help but it was 5:15 in the morning and no one was going to be awake to help me. I decided to do what she said and went back to bed.

When I got up again a few hours later I knew what I had to do. I quickly sent out an SOS text to all the women I knew, including Casey asking them to meet me at the clubhouse. I locked up Siobhan's house and rushed back to the clubhouse to shower and get ready for my impromptu meeting.

CHAPTER 13

Needles

I was in the kitchen making a pot of coffee with Alana, Brooke, Kat, Pixie and Casey walked in all talking. Ashlyn was even there with Pixie, the more help the better.

"So what the hell is going on here?" Casey demanded her hands on her hips.

"I need some help." I replied seriously. "There's something going on with Siobhan at work and she can't get any answers. I've asked Lo to look into it for me but in the meantime," I held up Siobhan's key for them to see, "what does this mean?"

"Is that the key to her house?" Kat demanded leaning forward in her chair.

"Yeah, she gave it to me this morning as she ran out the door to work." I sighed just as Lo, Axle and Hammer walked into the kitchen and sat beside their women. "Oh fuck."

"What's going on?" Seether asked as he stepped in the room a few seconds after the others.

"SOS meeting," Pixie answered, kissing Seether once he'd settled her on his lap in her chair.

"What does that mean?" Axle asked his face a mask of confusion as he turned to Brooke. She smiled indulgently and patted his cheek.

"This have to do with that text about Siobhan's job?" Lo asked leaning back in his chair, his hand dangling down beside him and rubbing Alana's ankle.

"Yes and no," I replied shrugging. I explained what Siobhan had told me last night with a little help filling in details from Casey and ended with Siobhan giving me the key to her house. "I'm just confused and she's going through so much right now I really don't want to bombard her with questions."

"Ask Lachy," Brooke suggested shrugging. "If anyone knows Siobhan it's her brother, is he busy right now? Drag him in here."

"I'll get him," Axle said, jumping up and leaving the room.

"So this isn't her asking you to move in?" Hammer asked looking at me then at Kat.

"No, I don't think so." I answered shaking my head. "I wondered that at first, too but no, Siobhan would have said that. She didn't say anything about me moving stuff in, she only said it would be easier for me to come and go."

"If she didn't say the words move in with me then that is not what she meant." Lachlan said as he walked into the room. "What the fuck is going on with her?"

Casey and I explained again what was happening at work and with Dean and Lachlan snorted angrily.

"She didn't even tell me, I had to find out her third day in the pool what the hell happened the hard way." Casey said, shrugging. Then she told us about radioing Siobhan on her radio and getting someone else. "I texted her because she was supposed to be on shift and she said she was, just not in her cruiser and not driving. I guess whichever car she was in at the time had a bleeder and puker the night before and she was stuck cleaning it up."

"That's disgusting," Ashlyn said wrinkling her nose. Everyone looked over at her and she shrugged, "It is disgusting." None of us could disagree with her.

"So, what am I going to do?" I asked finally looking around the room at my friends, my chosen family.

"Am I allowed to leave here?" Lachlan said suddenly, "With a chaperone?"

"Yeah, I guess," Brooke said and I shrugged.

"Then let's go. Ladies, you're going with Needles to clean the house and do some laundry, someone else is coming with me to get some groceries." Lachlan said walking out of the room. "Let's go, get the lead out!"

Siobhan

I walked into my house at the end of my shift, three hours later than I should have been to an immaculately clean house and the most wonderful scents I had ever smelled. Jaxon was sitting on my couch watching TV, just hanging out.

"What did you do?" I demanded, dropping my bag at the door.

"You were exhausted last night," He said shrugging, "I thought you could use a little help, the house is clean, the laundry is done and supper will be ready in about half an hour."

"You did my laundry?"

"Well, I had help from Lachlan but yeah and the girls at the club helped."

"You had Alana and Brooke and all the girls over here to help you clean my house?"

"There wasn't a lot to do, it's a small house." He shrugged, the look on his face was beginning to get a bit apprehensive.

"Holy fuck, thank you so much," I gushed, falling onto the couch beside him and pulling him down so I could kiss him.

"Gross, stop that!" I jumped up off the couch and spun around.

Lachy was standing in my kitchen with oven mitts and an apron on. "Geez, I go to the bathroom for five minutes and come back to a damn orgy!" he groused then smiled.

"Lachy," I breathed, putting my hands over my lips, feeling my eyes tear up. He looked amazing. He had gained weight and muscle and he looked so healthy.

"Hey sis," he said holding his arms out to the side so I could hug him.

"Oh my God!" I exclaimed, rushing into his arms. His chest was so solid underneath my cheek and he had gained so much weight that my hands couldn't touch around his back. He smelled so good and clean, his eyes were bright and not from drugs. His skin was healthy and pink and his blond hair was shiny and golden like it was supposed to be, not greasy and dirty. "You look so good! How do you feel?"

"Like a new person," he said then looked up as Jaxon cleared his throat. "I know Needles, I know I have a long way to go yet and this is just the start, but yeah, I do feel really good."

"It's completely out of your system?" I asked him, stepping back and holding his hands, looking him over.

"Yeah, detox sucked but I think it's gone. I still crave it but it's not like I have the opportunity to get it at the center. This is the first time I've been off the MC's grounds." Lachy watched me and his eyes teared up. "Fuck it's so good to see you."

Lachlan wrapped his arms around my shoulders and held me tight to his chest. I could feel the tears slipping from his eyes soaking the shoulder of my t-shirt and I let my own tears fall unchecked down my cheeks. I had my baby brother back.

"Thank you so much," Lachy whispered in my ear. "Thank you for never giving up on me. I love you so much sis." He held me so tight and kissed the side of my head.

"I've missed you so much over the last couple of years." I said, deciding now was not the time to hold back with him. I lifted my hands and bracketed them around his face, staring into his eyes, not letting him look away from me. "I lost you, you disappeared into that scared, hurt little boy and I couldn't find you. I am so sorry for what happened, that I couldn't change it or stop it, I am so sorry I failed you."

"You didn't fail me, sis. I failed myself. I wasn't strong enough to deal with what happened and mom and dad didn't know what to do with an angry, hurt boy." He said, shaking his head. "I failed me; the system that let that kind of person around little kids failed me, but never you. You have never, ever failed me."

"I'm so glad to have you back," I laughed through my tears and pulled him back into a tight hug. "Did you cook for me?"

"Hell yeah I did, I forgot buried under the drug how much I loved it." He said, pulling away from me and walking back into the kitchen.

I turned around to find Jaxon standing a few feet away with his hands in his pockets. The look on his face was tight, like he was worried but I didn't know what he would have to be worried about. I rushed over to him and through my arms around his neck and hugged him so hard. His own arms came up and held me to him like he never wanted to let go.

"Thank you so much for giving me back my brother." I whispered, letting my tears flow again.

"I didn't do anything," He whispered, kissing my neck, "I only made sure he couldn't get any more drugs, he did all the rest."

"Still," I said, shaking my head and leaning back to look into his eyes, God he had beautiful eyes. "If it wasn't for you agreeing to take Lachy on he never would have gotten where he is now."

"He's got a long road still ahead of him," Jaxon warned.

"I know, but this is the brother who would fight for anything. This is the brother I had before that man came into our lives and ripped us apart. You were part of giving that back to me, I love you."

Jaxon sucked in a breath and stared down at me. "Do you love me because of Lachlan?"

"No," I said smiling and shaking my head. "I love you because you're a good person, because you take care of me, because you go out of your way to make me feel good. And because of what you did for Lachlan but not because of Lachlan himself. You're right, he did this himself, he made the right choice but he wouldn't have if he wasn't given the option and you gave him that option. You gave him that option because of your own inner strength to live through hell and come out the other side and give me heaven."

I pulled him down and kissed him again, controlling the kiss as I pushed my tongue past his lips to taste him and try to convince him that I loved him for him and not for anything connected to Lachy. It didn't take long before he was taking over the kiss, pulling me tight against him and burying his hand in my hair, tilting my head so he could completely control me.

"Stop!" Lachy called from the kitchen, "Supper's ready!"

CHAPTER 14

Siobhan

So my job didn't suddenly get better because my brother was clean and working on his recovery. My job didn't get better because Jaxon was staying at my house most nights and got up with me every morning and made me coffee to take to work.

My job still seriously sucked but I always had something to look forward to at the end of the day. Jaxon was always there waiting when I walked in the front door. Once again he had changed his schedule so he could spend evenings with me, perks of being the boss he said.

I had told him a week before that I loved him and he hadn't said it back, but that was ok. I didn't need the words; his actions said so much more than his words ever could. I was still having problems at work.

The other guys that I worked with were still using my desk as a lunch table and I was still getting the worst of the jobs and I was about to complain to my supervisor when I showed up at work and was handed transfer papers again. This time I was moving my box of things to the bylaw office.

As I stood in the elevator to go up the two flights to my new office I pulled out my personal cell phone and texted Jaxon.

Got transferred again, up to bylaw

Y were u transferred now?

Don't know, haven't ever been told the why,

Just told to go.

I askd Lo to look in2 it, he has connections
I'll ask him again, see if he herd nething

Thanks, but I don't think it will matter.

Never no, I'll let u no what he says

By the time I finished texting with Jaxon I was at the reception desk of the bylaw division. I placed my box on the desk and told the receptionist why I was there. It was all of seven in the morning and I was already exhausted.

"Oh," She said, shuffling through papers on her desk. "That's so weird, we were expecting you last week."

"What? How were you expecting me last week when I was only told this morning I was being transferred?"

"I don't know how these things work, I'm just a receptionist but you can certainly talk to our commander when he's free." She pointed over to the commander's office where I could see him laughing with none other than Dean. Fucking fantastic.

"Whatever," I said irritably, "Can you just show me which desk I can use and what I need to get to work on?"

"Oh of course," the lady said cheerfully, buzzing me back behind the desk. I went through the door and set my box of things on the desk she pointed to that was covered in files.

"Whose files are these?" I asked, looking up at her.

"They're yours of course, like I said we expected you last week. You're a little behind." She smiled and turned back to her own work as I slumped into my chair. I was opening the file on top of the pile when Dean sat in the chair beside my desk.

"So, you done yet?" He smirked at me.

"What?"

"You heard me," He replied, that smarmy look still on his face.

"So you're admitting now that you're doing this? Getting me transferred in and out of departments and having me do the shittiest jobs?" I said holding up the file in my hand about a dog fighting operation.

He shrugged but didn't say anything, instead standing and walking out of the office as he chuckled to himself.

"See you later, baby!" Dean called over his shoulder.

"MacDonald!" I snapped to attention at the sound of the commander calling me from his office. I jumped up and rushed over, stopping at the threshold until I was invited in. "You're a week late!"

"Yes sir, I was not informed until this morning that I was being transferred again."

"It looks like you're difficult to work with."

"Sir?"

"You being transferred so much? You have a problem with authority? Or working with others?"

"No sir, my record has always been exemplary. I neither asked for these transfers nor expected them sir."

"Uh huh, well just do your job and keep your nose clean and we shouldn't have any problems." He said snorting like he didn't believe me. "I suggest you get through as many as those files on your desk as you can and quickly. Being a week late has set you back a lot and some of those files are time sensitive."

"Yes sir." I said but didn't move.

"You're dismissed MacDonald."

"Yes sir." Now I turned and left the office, my hands shaking with fury.

I decided I'd had enough. It was time to make an appointment with HR. Unfortunately it would be another two weeks before I could get an appointment with HR and until then I was stuck working in the bylaw office.

Needles

I was sitting in Lo's office, listening to him talking on the phone to someone over at the detachment. He didn't sound happy either. From this end it was a pretty one sided conversation. When Lo finally hung up the phone he sighed tiredly and rubbed his eyes.

"Holy fuck your girl pissed someone off." Lo said resting back in his chair. "I don't know what's actually going on, but according to her file with HR she's requested all these transfers. They even have her signature on the transfer papers and the request forms."

"No fucking way," I muttered shaking my head. "Siobhan loved her job, she would never request a transfer and definitely not into the motor pool, bylaw maybe, or K9 but not motor pool."

"Well, I don't know what to tell you man, I believe you and her that she would request these transfers but I don't know what's going on and my influence ends with asking a few questions." Lo replied holding his hands in the air in an exaggerated shrug just as my phone beeped with an incoming text. I pulled it out to find a very angry looking message all in capital letters from Siobhan.

**THEY TRANSFERRED ME A WEEK AGO AND
DIDN'T TELL ME UNTIL TODAY! I HAVE 3
WEEKS WORTH OF WORK SITTING ON MY
DESK AND MOST OF IT IS TIME SENSITIVE!! WTF
DID I DO TO DESERVE THIS?**

**Fuck baby, I don no, lo jst fnd out hr
Has your sign. On req. and transf. papers.**

NO FUCKING WAY! I WOULD NEVER REQUEST

A TRANSFER! AND ESPECIALLY NOT TO MOTOR POOL!!

I no, we'll figure it out, I prmse

AARRGGHHHH!!!!

That was the last I heard from Siobhan until later that day when she came home, three hours late. Turns out her shift with bylaw was eight to four thirty, not six to two thirty like the motor pool. And of course no one mentioned that to her until she said good-bye to the receptionist, getting ready to leave for the day. Siobhan was a little pissed.

I was sitting on her couch when she slammed through the front door, angrier than I'd ever seen her before.

"It was Dean!" she exclaimed before I could say anything. "When I got to the bylaw office he was there talking to the commander and actually admitted, though not in so many words, that he was the one behind it all. What the hell am I supposed to do?"

"File a grievance? Sue him?"

"Right, sue a lawyer? Even if I had the money for that I wouldn't know the first thing to getting started." She said shaking her head and slumping onto the couch beside me. "By the way, your spelling sucks."

I snorted at her and smiled, "I know, sorry. Why don't I call Sharpie, the MC's lawyer and he can figure this all out for you?"

"Really? He would do that for me?"

"Fuck baby, you're mine, that means you're the clubs, hell yeah he'd do that for you." I retorted, pulling her into my arms.

"That doesn't help with the money part, though. I have some saved but not enough to stand up to a lawyer who plays dirty."

"Use mine," I shrugged.

"What,"

"Seriously, my parents started a trust fund for me when I was a kid. I've never used it, I'm sure there's more than enough money there to get Dean to fuck off."

"You're nuts," she said, shaking her head moving to stand but I grabbed her hand and pulled her down into my lap.

"Stop it, I love you and you're hurting, that means I'm hurting. If it's going to cost me a little money to make it better than fine, I'll pay it, I don't care." I said seriously, gripping her chin with my hand, holding her so she had to look into my eyes.

"You love me?"

"Fuck Siobhan, of course I do!" I exclaimed, quickly flipping her so she was lying underneath me on the couch. "I love you more than anything. You are mine and I will do everything I can to make this better for you. If you want me to step back and let it play out I will but it will kill me to do it. Please let me call Sharpie and help you."

She watched me for a long time, her gaze shifting over my face and back to my eyes before she finally nodded. I leaned down and kissed her, trying to show her without words just how much I loved her.

"Move in with me?" She asked when I finally pulled back to kiss a trail down her throat, both of us panting. I reared back to look into her eyes, "I mean if you want to, you're practically here all the time anyway and I hate it when you're not, but if you don't want to then don't feel obligated to."

"Shut up Siobhan," I said and kissed her hard again, "I'd love to move in with you."

I levered off the couch, pulling her with me and dragged her to the bedroom where I made love to her until we both fell back exhausted and sated.

CHAPTER 15

Siobhan

"Well," Sharpie said sitting back in his desk chair after hearing my story. "This is rather complicated. Dean Zane is a dick, no doubt about it. I suggest that besides filing a grievance you also file a protection order."

I nodded, as a police officer I knew what the process was.

"What does that entail?" Jaxon asked, looking from me to Sharpie.

"I need proof that Dean is causing me problems. That's going to be hard; he's a lawyer he has every right to be at the detachment." I said sighing and tipping my head back to look at the ceiling.

"Well, the detachment must have cameras right?" Jaxon asked again his gaze shifting from me to Sharpie. "Are we allowed access to them to prove that Dean could be involved?"

"We could ask for a court order," Sharpie said shrugging, "But depending on the judge that might not get us anywhere."

"So what do we have to do now?" Jaxon asked us, always wanting all the information he can get.

"We go to court," Sharpie replied matter of fact, "It's a process that we have to follow. I'll get it all going and make sure everything is as it should be. Siobhan just needs to write out everything she can remember from the time this all started to the present. And I mean everything."

"I know," I said nodding, no matter how embarrassing I found something I had to reveal it to the court and all the people there.

I had to believe it was worth it and until something came of all of this I would continue to go to work at the bylaw office and do my job to the best of my ability. I had a good reputation where it counted; anyone who knew me would say so.

"Is it possible that Zane could have gotten a copy of your signature?" Sharpie asked now, scratching his chin.

"I suppose it's possible," I said, shrugging. "He had been to my house once; I suppose he could have gotten a hold of my files or sensitive paperwork. And he is a lawyer, he has access to people who can forge and break and enter."

"This is true," Sharpie replied, obviously thinking of something. I let him think and Jaxon and I got up to leave, thanking Sharpie as we went. I still had a meeting with HR today and I had to get over to the detachment quickly.

Jaxon was waiting for me in the lobby when I left my meeting with HR an hour later. He had a hot coffee in his hand that he gave to me and smiled.

"How'd it go?" He asked, kissing my cheek as I took the first sip of the hot beverage.

"Eh," I said, shrugging. "The head of the department said she'd look into my claims but without proof that's all I've got, claims." Jaxon took my hand and we walked outside into the frigid November air. "She pointed out that it is my signature on those request forms and I swore to her that it couldn't be unless it was a forgery and she seemed perplexed by that but who knows if she actually believed me."

"Well let's go get something to eat, Bold Pizzeria sound good?" Jaxon asked as he led me to his truck. He had put his bike into storage for the winter and he wasn't too happy about it. Especially when we got to his truck and found two of his tires slashed. "What the fuck? I'm parked in a police station parking lot and my tires are slashed? There's got to be video out here right?"

"Uh, yeah there should be." I said turning to walk back into the detachment to talk to one of the clerks there. Two hours later, the parking lot surveillance was watched and reviewed and we had no more information.

Whoever it was who slashed Jaxon's tires knew where the cameras were and was careful not to look at them or even in their direction and he kept his head covered. That's about all we knew, the person who did the slashing was a man.

"Fuck!" he exclaimed now as we stood and looked down at his tires. "I guess I'll call a tow truck, sorry about supper baby."

"It's fine Jaxon, why don't we get a cab back to my place and get my car, then we can go out and pick up pizza and take it home while your truck is taken out to the clubhouse?"

"Yeah I guess," he sighed, rubbing a hand over his head. I called Chrissy at the Pizzeria and ordered our pizza's then waited with Jaxon until the tow truck showed up to take his truck to the clubhouse. As we were waiting he got a phone call that made him see red.

Needles

I was standing with Siobhan waiting for the tow truck when my phone rang. As I pulled it out of my pocket to answer it stopped ringing then started again. That was strange but I saw it was Lix's phone that was calling. Lix didn't make phone calls since he couldn't hear.

"Hello?" I asked, wondering who the hell had Lix's phone.

"Needles? It's me Ash, are you busy right now? Can you come down to the shop?" Ashlyn asked and she sounded very upset.

"Uh yeah I'm just waiting on a tow truck, then we'll catch a cab right over. What's wrong?"

"Um, well Lix and I were just leaving the shop and locking up when a car drove past and threw a brick through the window." Ashlyn said and her voice started to get shrill.

"Did you call the police?"

"Yeah, but that's not it." She replied and I could hear the sobs starting in her chest. "There were two bricks thrown, one went through the window and the other hit Lix in the head. He's unconscious. I called 911 on my phone and then took his out of his pocket and called you. I'm sitting out in front of the shop alone with an unconscious man lying across my lap and it's getting dark and it's cold and I'm really scared."

"Ok, Ash just hang on, I'll send out a message and see if any of the other guys are in the area and can meet you there and stay with you. Don't worry, someone will be there soon. Siobhan and I are getting a cab now and we'll be there ASAP, ok?"

"Ok Needles, I'll wait,"

"Are you still on the line with the 911 operator?" I asked, looking at Siobhan as she pulled her own phone out and called Casey.

"Yeah, she's talking to someone else now but she's still there." Ashlyn replied, sniffing. "Oh, Casey just came on the line . . . ok Casey, yeah I'm ok . . . yeah I can hear the sirens now . . . thanks Casey. Needles?"

"Yeah Ash, I'm still here."

"The ambulance and the police are here now; they just pulled up in front of the shop. I gotta go, the police want to know if you're coming here or going to the hospital first?"

"Tell them I'll meet you all at the hospital ok? You be strong for Lix ok Ash?"

"Ok Needles, see you soon?"

"Yeah sweetheart, we'll see you soon. I'll call Pixie too and get her to call your dad ok?"

"Thanks Needles see you soon," And she hung up.

"FUCK!" I yelled into the dark sky.

"Casey said to take her car; I have an extra set of keys so we don't have to call a cab." Siobhan said, pulling me towards the parking garage of the detachment and handing me a set of keys from her purse. "We'll get there faster this way."

We found Casey's SUV and climbed in then drove much faster than we should have to the hospital. Luckily we were only a few blocks from the hospital and made it there faster than the ambulance taking Lix. We stayed in the emergency waiting room until we saw Ashlyn come through the doors behind the EMTs.

"Needles!" She cried rushing over to us. I wrapped her in my arms and we waited as patiently as possible for news. Ashlyn's sister Pixie and her dad arrived a little while later just in time for us to be called by the doctor.

"I'm Felix's boss," I said stepping forward, "He doesn't have any family."

"Ok, well Mr. Taggart has sustained a concussion, it's not a major one but it's more than a minor concussion. He's going to need to be watched for a few days to make sure the symptoms don't get worse. Other than that he is a very lucky young man."

"Thank you doctor," I said as the man nodded and walked away.

"I would say Lix should come home with us but I only have one bedroom." Siobhan said looking up at me.

"Why doesn't he come home with me and Aiden?" Pixie asked, looking at each of us. "That way we can keep an eye on him and he's with someone he knows and is comfortable with. Plus Aiden knows sign language and I'm learning so we can communicate with Lix. And Uncle James doesn't have to worry about Ash sneaking into Lix's room."

James just snorted but agreed and Ashlyn looked relieved that Lix would be going somewhere safe.

"Also Needles," Pixie said, turning to me, "Aiden is already going over the security video from the shop, hopefully he can get something for you."

"Thanks Pix," I said nodding. We all turned as Lix was wheeled out to us in a wheelchair with a bandage on his head.

"I can go home!" he shouted to us. He didn't know he was yelling so we all smiled and I made the sign for 'quieter'. He got the point and moved to sign language. I had a feeling the ringing in his ears was worse than usual.

"Pixie if you can take Lix to your house Siobhan and I will go back to the shop and talk to the police there and get the broken window boarded up." Pixie agreed and we all left, Ashlyn came with us to pick up her car and then head over to Pixie and Aiden's place.

When we got to the shop we learned it was much worse than we thought. The brick that had gone through the window had gone through my main window, completely shattering it. I had been meaning to get the window replaced with a double pain but hadn't had the chance.

Now I didn't have a choice, and since I was putting out the money for a new window I might as well get the shop's name painted on it. Not worth the pain my friend and employee was suffering, that's for sure.

The police asked a few questions about whether or not I had any enemies, which I didn't and if I knew of anyone who would do this. Again, I didn't. Siobhan talked to the cops for a few minutes after they'd asked their questions and we promised to send over the security footage in the morning. Then I went to the back of the shop to look for something to board up the window with.

"Hey," Siobhan said, coming back to find me. "I just got a call from Chrissy; I totally forgot that we ordered pizzas. Why don't I go pick them up and bring them back here?"

"That's a fucking fantastic idea." I told her as my stomach rumbled. I pulled her into my arms, "But first this . . . "I kissed her deeply, taking control of her mouth and sucking on her tongue, nipping her lips. "Go get my pizza woman, and then tonight I'm going to love you until you can't walk."

"Mm," she moaned into my mouth, "I can't wait." She kissed me once more hard then turned and left.

CHAPTER 16

Needles

The next day I called a glass company to come and replace my window. It was way more fucking expensive than I thought it would be. I almost choked on my tongue when the guy passed me the bill. I sighed and pulled out my checkbook and wrote a check for the full amount and set the bill aside to send to the insurance company just as my phone rang.

"Hey Sharpie, what's up?" I asked as I answered.

"Well, I don't suppose Siobhan's around is she?"

"Nope, I'm at the shop signing over my first born to pay for the window that was broken last night, she's at home."

"I heard about the shit last night," Sharpie said and I could hear the tightness in his jaw. "Can I meet you at Siobhan's place? In say twenty minutes? I've got some news."

"Sure man, is this good news or bad?"

"It's not good news Needles."

"Fuck, ok give me half an hour to get home and prepare her."

"All right man, see you soon." Sharpie said and hung up. I locked up the shop and headed home to Siobhan.

The day after she had asked me to move in with her I started bringing my stuff over to her place. I really only had clothes to move and my stereo and TV. There wasn't anywhere in Siobhan's house to put my bed so I left it at the clubhouse and switched Siobhan's TV with mine since mine was newer and bigger.

She shrugged when I did it and I knew she wouldn't care since she only watched TV if I was with her anyway. I did squeeze my dresser into her room, though. Her dresser wasn't big enough for both of our clothes and even after I hung my shirts in her closet I needed more than a little space in her dresser.

Again she shrugged and smiled then kissed me on the lips and left for work. Now I drove home, to our house knowing I was about to prepare her for bad news, not knowing just how bad it was. Sharpie sounded pissed more than worried but that didn't mean I wasn't worried.

"Hey baby," Siobhan said when I stepped in the front door. "You're home earlier than I thought you'd be."

"Yeah," I sighed, closing the door behind me. I walked over to where she was standing at the kitchen counter and wrapped my arms around her waist. "I got a call from Sharpie, he's on his way over."

"Oh?" She turned in my arms and wrapped hers around my neck. "What's he got to say?"

"He didn't tell me, just said it wasn't good news. I asked him to give me a few minutes to prepare you." I said locking my gaze with hers. "No matter what he says, baby we'll figure it out, ok?"

"Yeah Jaxon, we will figure it out." She said smiling up at me. "I've been thinking a lot about this. I love being a cop, but recently it's become more of a trial than a love. I don't want to let Dean win but I also don't want to spend all my time fighting him and trying to keep my head above water. If this doesn't work out then I'm just going to leave the force and find something else to do."

"I hate that you've come to that," I sighed, resting my forehead on hers and closing my eyes. "I know how much you love being an officer; I know how hard that decision was for you. I really hope it doesn't come to that."

"Me too," She shrugged as the doorbell rang, "But that's what I'm prepared to do."

I kissed her lightly on the lips and went to answer the door. Sharpie was there looking like the lawyer and not the biker. We shook hands and I welcomed him into the house. Siobhan came into the living room with a tray of coffee cups and a pot of fresh coffee. She placed it on the coffee table then gave Sharpie a quick hug.

"All right," She said, taking a deep breath, "What's the damage?"

Siobhan

"Well, we filed for a protection order against Zane, and he filed a counter order." Sharpie said, taking a sip of the coffee I had poured for him.

"What?" Jaxon demanded, jumping to his feet. "What the fuck?"

"Unfortunately he's well within his rights to do so." Sharpie said shaking his head, "However he's stating in his brief that Siobhan is stalking him and he has video proof. He hasn't turned his evidence over yet so we can't have discovery but we have turned all of our evidence over and so far the judge is leaning in our favor."

"I figured Dean would do something like this," I replied shrugging. "He's so slimy, I'm really not surprised."

"It's fucking ridiculous." Jaxon exclaimed pacing from the front door to the kitchen and back again. My house was so small he only went about ten steps in either direction before turning again.

"Well there is something else," Sharpie said sitting forward. "Whoever it was who slashed your tires didn't wear gloves, so we might be able to get a match on the prints left on the fender of your truck. Either that or one of the bricks thrown at the shop, if

Zane was involved first hand in either one of those incidents then we can have him arrested for vandalism and assault since one of those bricks hit Lix."

"Well, that's something at least." I said looking up into Jaxon's angry face.

"I've closed the shop for the next couple of days," Jaxon said sitting beside me. "I rescheduled the appointments we had on the books for next week so I'll be around to keep an eye on you for a couple of days."

"I'm glad," I said smiling at Jaxon. We visited with Sharpie for a few more minutes, making plans and just talking and then he got up and left us alone. Jaxon was sitting in the corner of the couch and I curled up against him, pulling my legs under me. We sat that way for a few minutes as he played with my hair and we just enjoyed each other's company.

"Take me to bed," I said, sitting up and locking my gaze with his.

The smile on Jaxon's face was immediate and wide. I stood and pulled him to stand with me then led him into the bedroom behind me. Once I stood beside my bed I turned to him and started undoing the buttons on his shirt.

He reached out to put his hands on my hips and I swatted them away. He smirked at me but I kept at his buttons until I could push his shirt off his shoulders and onto the floor.

I looked up at him and pulled him down for a kiss but as soon as he tried to take over I pulled away then unbuckled his belt and pulled the button of his pants loose, then dragged his zipper down and his pants over his hips.

Jaxon's eyes were dark with passion, his pupils so dilated I almost couldn't see the brown around the edges. Then I pushed him to sit on the bed and I knelt in front of him and pulled off his boots and socks. When his feet were bare I grabbed the hem of his jeans and pulled until he sat before me naked.

His cock was hard and jutting and I licked my lips thinking of how much I wanted it in my mouth. Jaxon growled when my tongue peeked through my lips and reached for me. I wasn't ready to give up control though and I swatted his hands away again, pushing him to lie back on the bed. I smoothed my hands up his thighs and gripped his hips, flexing my fingers into his muscles. I leaned forward and licked Jaxon's cock from base to tip, then swirled my tongue around the head and through the crease at the tip.

"Fuck baby," he moaned clenching his hands into fists.

Just as he reached to grip my hair I swallowed his cock, taking him as deep as I could into my mouth and when I felt him touch the back of my throat, swallowed. I pulled back slightly as he sat up and rested on his elbows to watch me.

I looked up at him and gave him a wicked smile and saw his hair was a mess where he must have shoved his hands through it. Before he could do anything I kissed the head of his cock and stood, backing up a step.

"Baby?"

I shook my head at him and slowly pulled my t-shirt over my head, letting my hair slowly fall around my shoulders. Jaxon sat up all the way and reached for me again but I took another step back and dropped my shirt to the floor.

I clutched the waistband of the leggings I had put on that morning and started to slowly push them down my hips, a little on each side at a time, crouching as I followed my pants down then slipped them off my feet.

When I stood again I reached behind me and undid the clasp on my bra, pulling off and dropping it to the floor with my shirt. When I was completely naked I stepped forward again and straddled Jaxon's lap, taking his cock in my hand and holding him as

I sunk down on him, squeezing him with my inner muscles as I went.

"Holy fuck baby," He whispered when he was fully seated inside me.

I hadn't said a word or made a sound since we had come into the bedroom and now I bit my lower lip as I started to undulate my hips, rubbing my clit against his hard stomach.

"I can't . . . please baby, let me take over . . ."

Before I answered him I tossed my head back and let my hair brush his thighs as I arched my breasts into his face. He moaned and leaned forward, dragging one of my nipples into his mouth and sucking hard. Jaxon's hands slid up my back and gripped my shoulders as he started to thrust hard up into me. I finally looked down at him and told him, I hoped, with my eyes that he could and should take what he wanted, what he needed.

CHAPTER 17

Needles

Once I started thrusting and Siobhan looked at me, so much love and acceptance in her eyes I knew she was ready to give up control. I stood quickly and flipped our positions, laying her gently on the bed, careful not to pull out of her as I loomed over her.

She lay under me panting and I leaned forward and kissed her hard, pushing my tongue into her mouth and tasting her everywhere. Soon my tongue was mimicking the movements of my hips and she was whimpering and pushing her hips into mine.

I reached down and gripped her thigh, pulling it up and bending her knee, wrapping my arm around her leg to keep her as open to me as possible. I was able to thrust impossibly deeper, making her pull her mouth from mine and cry out.

Her inner muscles flexed and tightened around my cock as I drove into her and then her hand was sneaking between us to rub her clit. Instead of rubbing though she just placed her fingers over it and let my thrusting rub for her.

It didn't take long then before she was arching and crying out and her orgasm started to milk my cock and just as I was about to cum I realized I wasn't wearing a condom.

"No!" I shouted and pulled out of her, arching over her as I spilled my cum all over her stomach. She moaned again as my hot seed washed over her and she looked down at the mess panting. "Fuck, sorry." I said pulling away from her but she wouldn't let me go.

Instead she pulled me down so hard I landed on top of her, spreading my cum all over both of us. She leaned up and grasped the back of my head and kissed me hard on the mouth, sliding her tongue between my lips and licking the roof of my mouth and moaning.

"That was fucking hot." She whispered against my lips then smiled, "But now I think we both really need a shower." I looked down at the sticky mess that was between us and laughed.

"Yeah, I think that's a good idea."

Over the next week as Siobhan worked at the bylaw office catching up on the files that had been stacked on her desk I cleaned up at the shop. It really didn't take long since only the front window was really damaged, or so I thought. Every day I showed up at the shop there was something else that needed to be fixed.

The first day it was spray paint across the new window, the second it was crazy glue in the lock on the front door. The third day was the worst though with paper bags left flaming on the front step. I could just imagine what was in the bags so instead of stomping the flames out I threw the freshly fallen snow on them to put the flames out.

My shop neighbours on the street were starting to get worried. They didn't know that I was being targeted specifically and they thought maybe they could be next. I tried to reassure them that it was highly unlikely that the person doing this to me would target them but they still worried.

The only thing I could tell them was to keep their security cameras on and be careful. I even offered to pay to put more security cameras on their stores and assured them I would be putting more up on mine as well.

Hopefully that way we could catch whoever this was. They all shook their heads and said not to worry, they would deal with their security but that I should for sure up mine.

I was putting up a new camera when Lix and Ashlyn walked up to the store the day before I planned to open again.

"You still having trouble?" Lix called up to me but I couldn't really answer him so I looked to Ashlyn and she nodded.

"Not since the day before yesterday." I said to her and she relayed it to Lix.

"Still gonna open tomorrow?" Lix asked her.

"Yup," I said and she nodded her head. I finished with the install of the camera and climbed down the ladder I was standing on. "You good to work tomorrow?" I asked him when my feet were on the ground.

"Hell yeah," Lix answered, nodding and giving me a fist bump. This kid was awesome.

"You too, Ashlyn? It's gonna get busy now close to Christmas." I said leading them into the store.

"Yeah, I can work tomorrow," she replied nodding. "I talked to my dad and he said it was ok if I worked here as long as it was safe."

"Your dad the dentist is ok with his daughter becoming a tattoo artist?" I asked looking between her and Lix.

"Yeah, he knows art is important to me and this is a way to make pretty good money with it. He doesn't want me tattooing my face or anything like that but he's good with it." She shrugged.

"Well, you will never be here by yourself and I just added more security so you should be completely safe. Just be smart when you leave at night, never go alone and leave the deposit for the morning." I said, happy to have a new employee and a female one at that.

I wasn't joking about things getting busy with Christmas only a few weeks away. This year had gone really quickly. I stood quietly watching Lix and Ash getting cozy with each other and thinking about Siobhan. I shook my head and went to the back of the store to set up the new cameras on the feed on my computer.

Siobhan

Jaxon texted me from the store to let me know that Lix was there and doing much better. I was really relieved as I'm sure Jaxon was as well. I smiled at the little emoji Jaxon sent and put my phone in the top drawer of my desk and got to work on my latest case. I don't know what it was that made people think dog fights were a great way to make money but I thought it was sickening.

"MacDonald!" I jumped when my commander called from his office. I rushed over and knocked on the door frame and waited to be called in. "Enter."

I pushed the door open and closed it quietly behind me then stood in front of the commander's desk and waited.

"I just got a request from you for a transfer, is this for real?"

"What? No sir, I did not request a transfer. As a matter of fact sir I didn't request the last two transfers." I said confused, shaking my head.

"Well MacDonald, this here form is signed by you; do you deny that this is your signature?"

"Yes sir I do deny it. I did not sign that request."

"I got a heads up from HR that there's something going on between you and Dean Zane."

"No sir, there is nothing going on between myself and Mr. Zane. We dated once, he did not like when I broke things off and he's been trying to make my life difficult ever since."

"Those are pretty serious charges, MacDonald." The commander said leaning back in his chair.

"Yes sir," I agreed.

"Do you have a lawyer, MacDonald?"

"Yes sir I do."

"For now I am going to shred this request for transfer. Do you like working here in bylaw MacDonald?"

"Yes sir, I do. I like being a Constable sir," I said still standing at parade rest.

"All right, if any more of these requests come across my desk I will talk to you first."

"Thank you sir," I said relieved that finally someone was talking to me.

"Dismissed." I turned and quickly left the Commander's office. Hopefully this meant things were looking up.

I had a surprise for Jaxon. I had decided that I was going to get a tattoo. I had actually decided to get one a couple of months ago but couldn't decide what it was I actually wanted.

I had searched websites directed to tattoo design, I had talked to Alana and Ashlyn and still I didn't know, but I had finally figured it out. I wanted something that showed off my Scottish heritage but also my love of the RCMP and my job.

I decided on a small set of bagpipes with a Mountie Stetson hanging off of one of the pipes. Behind the bagpipes would be half of the Scottish flag connected to half of the Canadian flag and hanging off of another of the pipes I wanted a grenade pin.

I thought having a needle tattooed on me might be a bit strange, but since Jaxon constantly carried around the grenade pin that would be less strange and still mean something to him.

I also wanted to be the first customer once he reopened after the window being broken. Actually I was going over there right after work today to have the tattoo done. He knew to wait for me there and I couldn't help but watch the clock. Just as I was starting to clean up my things and put my files away Dean slumped in the chair by my desk.

"You are not allowed to be here." I said as I stood planning on going straight to the Commander's office.

"Just sit down and hear me out," he said grabbing my wrist and squeezing it tightly.

"No, let me go." I said, trying to pull my arm away.

"Shut up, you are making this whole thing so much worse than it needs to be." Dean pulled me closer to him so that I almost fell into his lap.

"Stop! Let me go!" I was getting louder and louder knowing he would never just let me go. But instead he squeezed my wrist tighter, grinding the fine bones together with his fingers. "Ouch! Dean let me go!"

"Mr. Zane!" We both stopped struggling and turned when my Commander bellowed from his office door. "Do you have a purpose for being here right now?"

"No Commander," Dean sneered then turned to me, "I'm just leaving." Before he dropped my wrist she squeezed even tighter for a split second, spit "bitch," in my face and walked out of the office. I quickly cradled my injured wrist to my chest and watched him go.

"Are you alright MacDonald?"

"Yes Commander, I was just about to clock out." I replied, breathing heavily.

"You do that, and make sure to get that wrist checked out." The Commander turned back to his office. "I have a report to file, I expect you here in the morning to sign it." Then he closed his door and I was left alone with two other bylaw officers.

"Come on," Steve, one of the officers said, "I'll walk you to your car."

"Thanks," I smiled wearily up at Steve but didn't turn down his offer. I did not want to get caught alone in a parking garage with Dean if he decided he wasn't finished with me. I grabbed all my things and hurried out of the detachment, wanting to get to Jaxon as quickly as possible.

CHAPTER 18

Siobhan

The drive to the tattoo parlor didn't take long. I didn't bother to change out of my uniform before leaving the detachment since I wanted to get to Jaxon as quickly as possible. I parked my car in front of the shop and rushed inside carrying my bag with my clothes.

"Hey baby," Jaxon smiled as I stepped inside. He came around the counter and wrapped his arms around my waist and kissed me. "How was your day?"

"Good and bad, I've got a lot to tell you but I need to get changed first." I said smiling at him tiredly.

"Sure baby, use my office." He pointed me back to his office and I hurried over to the door, closing it behind me.

I changed as quickly as I could with my wrist so sore and getting worse as time went on. I really needed to get some ice on it and fast. I was ready to get back out to Jaxon but I couldn't tie my shoes with my wrist the way it was so I pulled the laces as tight as I could and tucked them into the side of my shoes.

"So, tell me the bad first," Jaxon said when I got back out of his office.

"Not yet, I have something I want to do first." I said getting excited. "Actually you have to do it."

"Uh, ok," He said looking down at me, confused. I pulled the drawing out of my back pocket that Ashlyn had done for me and handed it to him. "This is really cool."

"I want you to put it on my shoulder." I said smiling up at him.

"Really?"

"Yeah, I've been thinking about getting a tattoo for a long time but I really couldn't think of something that I wanted on my body forever. I sat down with Ash and between us we came up with that." I replied and shrugged.

"You want it done right now?"

"Yes please, I wanted to be your first customer when you opened again."

"This is so awesome, let's do it."

It took a couple of hours but as Jaxon worked I told him about my day, about my Commander calling me into his office and asking about yet another transfer request that I had supposedly signed.

Then I told him about Dean showing up just as I was about to clock out and how my Commander had stopped him from doing any real damage. That was when Jaxon stopped what he was doing and rolled his stool in front of me.

"What do you mean stopped him from doing any real damage?" he demanded crossly.

"Dean grabbed my wrist and squeezed it but he could have done much worse if my Commander hadn't come out of his office."

"Let me see."

"No, Jaxon I want you to finish my tattoo, I don't want to talk about a little bruise." Jaxon stared at me for a long time, trying to get me to change my mind. "Please, just finish and I'll show you after."

He finally relented and went back behind me to finish my tattoo. By then there wasn't much left and he was finished quickly. He pulled out a mirror and showed me the work and I smiled proudly up at him.

"Thank you so much, I love it." I said and lifted up on my toes to kiss him.

I turned away to get my wallet so I could pay for it, because I was going to pay for it whether he liked it or not, when I stepped on my shoe laces and tripped, falling into the table Jaxon had his equipment on. I cried out in pain as I hit my sore wrist but Jaxon caught me before I fell farther.

"Why aren't your shoes tied?" He demanded sitting me in a chair.

"I couldn't, my wrist hurt too much to tie them." I said shrugging.

"That's it, I'm taking you to the hospital."

"No, Jaxon,"

"Yes Siobhan, if it hurts so much that you can't tie your shoes then you need to see a doctor. Stop arguing, you're going."

"Fine," I said relenting and let him help me into my jacket and out to his truck.

"Once we're done at the hospital we're going back to the station and you're filing charges." Jaxon said angrily.

"I'm pretty sure my commanding officer is doing that. He told me he had a file to work on and I needed to be there to sign it in the morning."

"That's fine, but you still need to file charges on your own." Jaxon drove silently to the hospital and I was pretty sure I had never seen him this angry before, it was kind of scary.

We spent an hour in the ER, then another hour in diagnostics getting an x-ray and then back to the ER for another hour. My wrist wasn't broken but it was bruised enough that the doctor wanted me to wear a temporary plastic cast. It was ridiculous really but

Jaxon was so adamant that I do it so I didn't argue.

Then he ushered me back to the truck and drove back to the detachment where he watched and waited while I pressed charges for assault.

My Commander was called to give testimony as proof given that my case was rather unconventional with the assault happening in the detachment and that we already had matching protection orders against each other. With that done Jaxon took me home. I wasn't working the next day so leaving my car at the tattoo parlor was no big deal.

Jaxon

As soon as we got home I checked Siobhan's tattoo and sent her to bed. I was so angry about the whole situation that I just couldn't sleep yet. I paced around the living room wanting to punch something but instead called Sharpie to update him on what had happened.

He said he would immediately get to work on pushing for Dean's arrest now that he had actually caused physical harm to Siobhan in clear view of her coworkers.

Eventually I was relaxed enough I could at least take a shower in the hopes that the water would cool some of my anger. I stood under the spray for a long time before I felt I was under control enough to climb into bed with Siobhan and rest with her.

When I got to the bed she was lying on her side, facing away from me and her new tattoo was peeking out of the edge of the tank top she wore to bed. It was really a cool piece and I didn't miss the grenade pin hanging on the pipe of the bagpipe.

When I first saw it I thought I was going to tear up, loving that she would put a part of me on her body forever like that. I kissed her shoulder lightly and gathered her to me, pulling her back into my chest. She snuggled back and sighed then went back to sleep.

It was hours later when my phone rang from somewhere far away and I realized I had left it in the pocket of my jeans in the bathroom. After a minute it stopped ringing so I got comfortable again, planning on going back to sleep.

I looked over at the clock on the nightstand and saw that it was four in the morning. Too early for anyone to call just for the hell of it and when the phone started ringing again I knew something was wrong, and then Siobhan's phone started to ring.

I jumped up quickly and ran to the bathroom to grab my phone.

"Yeah, what?" I answered sharply.

"Oh my God, Needles it's about damn time you answered," Aiden said in my ear. "We've been trying yours and Siobhan's phones for the last hour. Where the hell have you been?"

"We were in bed," I replied looking up to see Siobhan step sleepily into the bathroom with her phone in her hand. It wasn't ringing anymore but she was scrolling through her list of missed calls. "What the hell is going on?"

"Ashlyn was attacked outside the tattoo parlor," Aiden rushed on, "It was Dean Zane, he beat her up pretty good before Lix got to her and stopped him. Lix went insane, he completely lost it, almost killed Zane. Both Zane and Ashlyn are in the hospital right now but Lix is being held at the detachment until further notice. Sharpie's already down there with him."

"Holy fuck," I breathed into the phone. "We'll get to the hospital as soon as we can." I said and hung up. Siobhan was looking up at me with confusion on her face.

"What-"

"Dean attacked Ashlyn, put her in the hospital, Lix caught him and almost killed him, put him in the hospital. Lix is being detained right now, we gotta go baby, right now, go get dressed."

I watched Siobhan's eyes widen and then she was running for the bedroom to get dressed. I grabbed my jeans off the floor and dragged them up my legs.

I couldn't find my shirt from earlier so I grabbed a long sleeved t-shirt out of my drawer and shoved the sleeves up to my elbows.

By the time I got to the living room Siobhan was ready and standing at the front door. As soon as she saw me she turned and rushed out the door to the truck.

I had grabbed a sweatshirt instead of a jacket, not wanting to take the time and met Siobhan in the truck then drove to the hospital, faster than I had ever driven anywhere.

When Siobhan and I got to the ER everyone was already there. Lo and Alana were standing in a corner of the room huddled up together talking quietly. Axle and Brooke were sitting in a chair together with Imogen on Brooke's lap sleeping.

Hammer and Kat were in much the same position but with three car seats at their feet. Pixie was sitting beside her uncle, her arm thrown over his shoulder talking quietly in his ear.

Her uncle's wife was missing but since she wasn't completely mentally well that wasn't a surprise. Seether was just stepping into the waiting room with trays of coffee for everyone.

Seether slapped me on the shoulder and jerked his head for me and Siobhan to follow him out to the hallway. When we got there and the door closed he turned to us with his hands on his hips and his head dropped then reached a hand up to rub the back of his head.

Seether was 6'8" so while he towered over most people he was a giant next to Siobhan.

"What's going on?" Siobhan demanded when Seether didn't speak right away.

"It's bad," He sighed looking up. "Ash and Lix had gone in to pick something up or drop it off I'm not sure but they were locking up and leaving when Lix realized he forgot something. He went back in and Ash stayed on the side walk. When Lix got back out she was gone. She said she was screaming as loud as she could but he couldn't hear her so it took him a few minutes to find her."

"Fuck," I breathed a heavy sigh, "He must be going fucking crazy."

"Yeah, so he finds them in the alley just as Zane is yanking her pants down, she's fighting like crazy and he's hitting her then ripping her pants then pulling at his own. Lix just reacted, he grabbed Zane and pulled him off Ash, threw him into a wall in the alley and beat the living shit out of him. Zane's here in the hospital, too but he's not quite as bad as Ash because she stopped Lix from killing him. Lix knocked Zane out just as Ash passed out then called 911."

"Where is Ashlyn now?" Siobhan demanded stepping towards Seether.

"She's up there somewhere getting stitched up and checked out." Seether said, shaking his head. "She's got a gash in her cheek and the bastard choked her so her throat's in rough shape. They thought maybe she had internal bleeding given how much Zane punched and kicked her in the midsection but she's got a few broken ribs."

"Is that her dad in there with Pixie?" Siobhan asked. Seether nodded and rubbed his hand over his face. "As a constable I have certain leverage here, do you think he would want me to find something out, get him in to see her sooner?"

"I'm sure he'd appreciate that, Siobhan." Seether said, sighing.

Siobhan turned and went back into the waiting room. There was a small window in the door and I could see her crouched in front of James Cameron, holding his hands as she spoke.

After a few minutes of nodding and talking she came back out again but didn't stop to talk, she went straight to the nurses station and flashed her badge.

CHAPTER 19

Siobhan

"Hi, I'm Constable Siobhan MacDonald, I'm here to talk to the assault victim from earlier tonight? Ashlyn Cameron?" I said to the nurse at the desk. She looked up at me with sympathy in her eyes and nodded, then consulted her charts.

"She's in room 12 there around the corner. The doctor is just finishing up his exam right now then she'll be moved to a private room." The nurse replied, pointing to the curtained area where Ash was being taken care of.

"Thank you, I'll be quick." I said and rushed around the corner. "Knock knock," I said since there wasn't anything to actually knock on.

Then I ducked my head inside the curtain to see Ashlyn laying on a bed with tears streaming down her cheeks.

"Constable MacDonald, I just need to ask the patient some questions." I said flashing my badge again.

"Sure," the doctor said nodding, "I'm almost finished here. I sure hope you get the guy who did this, he was quite brutal."

"Hey Ash," I said quietly, pulling a stool close to the bed.

"Siobhan?" she asked weakly, her voice raspy from being strangled.

"Yeah sweetie, can you tell me who did this to you?"

"I don't know his name." Ash cried, her tears flowing faster now.

"Can you describe him to me?"

"He was tall, but not as tall as Seether, like Lix and Needles. He had dark hair and I guess he was handsome, some people might think so I guess. He smelled like cologne and he wore a suit."

"Ok sweetie, I'm going to show you a couple of pictures, can you tell me if you recognize anyone?" Ashlyn nodded as I pulled my phone out of my pocket.

I had an old picture of Dean saved on my phone because he was standing in front of a particularly lovely sun set. I had been meaning to crop him out and hadn't gotten a chance to yet. I flipped through a few other photos of guys and girls from the MC and came to the one of Dean. Ashlyn grabbed my wrist, my casted wrist, and gripped me tightly.

"That's him! Siobhan, that's the guy." Ashlyn sobbed pointing at my phone.

"Ok Ash, I'm going to go and get your dad and Pixie ok, you just relax here and I'll send them in ok."

"Siobhan where's Lix, is he here? Can he come in, too?"

"I'll look for him ok," I said, not really lying but knowing Lix wouldn't be at the hospital anytime soon.

I rushed out of the room and down the hall to the waiting room. I opened the door and told Ashlyn's dad and Pixie that she wanted to see them and what room she was in then turned and ran back to the nurse's station.

I flashed my badge again and asked for Dean's room number. She gave it to me quickly and smiled again as I ran for the stairs. When I got to his floor I flashed my badge again at the nurses there and opened the door of Dean's room.

"Pardon me," I said interrupting the meeting he was having, sitting up in his bed. He had a black eye and a broken nose and there were bandages wrapped around his midsection. Lix had probably done some damage to his ribs, so sad. "Mr. Dean Zane you are under arrest for the assault and attempted rape of Ashlyn Cameron..."

Printed in Great Britain
by Amazon

86191938R00078